THE
MONSTER'S LEGACY

Books in the Dragonflight Series

THE
MONSTER'S LEGACY

ANDRE NORTON

Illustrated by
JODY A. LEE

A Byron Preiss Book

Atheneum Books for Young Readers

THE MONSTER'S LEGACY
Dragonflight Books

Atheneum Books for Young Readers
An imprint of Simon & Schuster Children's Publishing Division
1230 Avenue of the Americas
New York, NY 10020

Cover painting by Jody A. Lee. Cover design by Brad Foltz
Edited by Keith R. A. DeCandido & Nancy C. Hanger

Special thanks to Jonathan Lanman, Howard Kaplan, John Betancourt,
and Russell Galen.

First edition
Printed in the United States of America
10 9 8 7 6 5 4 3 2 1

ISBN 0-689-80731-7

Library of Congress Card Catalog Number: 95-80677

ACKNOWLEDGEMENTS

The author wishes to express her deep appreciation to Ms. Becky Peters, mistress of antique embroidery of the middle ages, without whose expert advice she might have gone woefully astray in several details.

1

Summer had come early to Var-The-Outer this year, bursting out with new life to banish all the sluggishness of winter from the hunting keep. It urged one out into the wide fields, even into the forested hills rising to the often mist-cloaked mountains beyond.

Sarita's gloved hands paused in that most delicate of tasks, winding finely beaten silver foil about a silken thread core. She could hear all the clamor below and at last could stand it no longer. Carefully setting aside the double-spooled frame, she went to the window.

When she leaned forward to peer through the narrow slit, she could see the riders gathering below. She told herself she was only trying to catch a glimpse of her own handiwork, the first piece she had finished that Dame Argalas had grudgingly admitted was worthy to be passed on to their patroness, the Countess Wanda.

Yes, that lady was wearing the fine green cloak with its overlay of silver patterning, so delicate it might be compared to the spiderwebs stretched on the field grass at early morning. Her own design, Sarita thought with a rise of pride, and her own stitchery—all her very own.

To be sure, she was within the last half season of her apprenticeship and near eight years of learning lay behind. So if she was any sort of a workwoman, she should be able to show a goodly measure of skill.

The countess was laughing; for the first time since their coming to this far holding a flush of color showed on her cheeks. She had been long recovering from a winter fever, drained and spent, lying abed most of the day. She had even lacked strength for little Lord

Valoris, now a sturdy child of more than two years. He had been large even at his birthing and had grown—as his nurse Halda declared often—like a weed ever since.

The earl had rejoiced in his son—though he did not see him often. And he was not unmindful of his lady (as Sarita well knew some lords could be), being greatly concerned when she did not throw off her persistent cough.

Full half the year she had kept to the bower. The wisewoman paid frequent visits with new potions, urging the countess to more exercise to restore her vigor. But their lady had complained of feeling ever tired, and the noise which arose from the huge bailey kept her awake; she could not breathe the thick air when winter kept them close to the hearth fires.

Once here in the outlands she had improved and took notice of Valoris. And lately she had called for Dame Argalas with questions concerning the work of the embroideresses-in-progress.

The next year would see the accession of the young High King to his full power. There would be a formal crowning in Raganfors. As one of the coregents, Earl Florian and his household would be much in view of all the city during the pageants, jousts, and ceremonies lasting for several weeks.

Accordingly there must be new banners, new trappings for all the jousting steeds, new ceremonial capes and robes—all certainly the finest possible. Two years earlier, Dame Argalas and her eldest and most accomplished apprentice had come to Castle Vars to set about the art of embellishing such examples of the earl's power and wealth.

Since by guild rules an embroiderer could only work by daylight, it had taken many weary hours and there were more to come. Still, Dame Argalas could take pride in what had already been accomplished.

She brought several samples of finished work to be shown to the countess. The countess had taken a liking to a certain pattern used on what was meant to be a minor robe and inquired concerning it. Sarita smiled, remembering Dame Argalas had not fancied that, but she was an honest woman and just and had brought forth Sarita, whose design it had been. So the countess had ordered a riding cloak for herself to be made by Sarita with a design the girl devised, though she had had to do it in spare moments, since her mistress had already set a schedule of tasks.

They had moved to Var-The-Outer—a small holding originally meant as a minor hunting lodge enlarged, by the countess' orders after her wedding, to be a place one could put off the formality of the great keep and be at peace.

And now there was a green cloak about the shoulders of the slender countess as she rode forth to oversee the lands for the first time. Her guards made a brave showing in their green-and-brown surcoats, the hunter-rangers all in green, their bows and quivers shouldered.

Sarita drew a longing breath—to be one of that party even for only part of a day! She suddenly wanted so much to be beyond all walls that she surprised herself. Hands holding reins, or gathering flowers in the meadows, were much better put to work embroidering if she was to escape one of the dame's icy scoldings.

She dropped down from the windowsill, where she had been standing on tiptoe, reluctantly returning to her stool and the infinitely delicate task of threadmaking, smoothing her thin gloves over her fingers—for the touch of skin against those threads could well dim them. It was tedious work and she would rather have been at the big embroidery frame at the other end of the chamber, stitching the pattern recently drawn there.

Dame Argalas was doubly talented in that she not only knew the most minute variations of stitchery, but she could also lay out patterns, a craft she had taught Sarita in its more simple phases. Usually the pattern-marked fabrics had to be bought from some artist, not left to the imagination of the one working out the design. But that was why Earl Florian had chosen the dame in the first place.

Through the half-open door, Sarita could now hear the scolding of Nurse Halda. Lord Valoris must have once more slipped his leash (which he too often did). He was a serious child, ever seeking new things.

There was a wail. The little lord had been either recaptured or deprived of some possession he had claimed for his own. Sarita had had little contact with so young a child before. She had been an only daughter, raised in guild fosterage, apprenticed at eight to

Dame Argalas. Certainly there had been no meddlesome children in *that* household—in fact, Sarita had been the youngest by several years.

She always feared now that Valoris might get loose in this workroom. Though she wore her tools at her waist, her scissors and the horn box of different grades of needles, as well as her punch awl, small, sticky, and often dirty hands could bring disaster to the work in progress. Yet one could not be cross with the child.

He was a beguiling mixture of his lady mother and the earl—the wide violet-blue eyes of the Countess Wanda, above a soft-fleshed but well-molded jaw which could set stubbornly on occasion. His always-tumbled hair was as golden as the long braid of the countess, but he would, Sarita was sure, grow to be as tall as his father.

And he was of a sunny nature, his pouting or whining rarely lasting long. He could be turned from a rage by showing him something curious. To tumble with the earl's prized hounds was his greatest joy, but one Halda deplored and kept him from as much as possible.

Sarita determinedly set to her task. Dame Argalas might not be there to offer barbed comment (she had journeyed with the earl to Raganfors these ten days past to see about the special dyings of certain cloths), but the girl had pride and she wanted her days stint to be fully accomplished—with perhaps a bit more. Still, when the breeze from the window ventured timidly in, she wished . . . for a time in the meadow without.

Rhys Fogarson drew a deep breath or two. Even the smell of horse—very strong—and the varied odors born of the clothing and the bodies of those about him could not damp that freshness for him. Those in the fore were raising dust on the trail now. It had been several ten-days since there had been any rain and this was a well-traveled path which, two days ahead, joined the great highway.

This was his first time to ride as a full-passed ranger and he knew those in his company who would seize at once on any awkwardness of bearing or uncalled-for speech. The newest ranger must always efface himself in public.

But he could sing inside and he did. The morn was so fine,

their company made a splendid sight, and, as all who had seen or known of her, he was glad that the countess had taken to horse once more, eager to ride. She had been so long a prisoner to her illness that some of the doubters had come to believe she would never venture out again at all.

His mount could easily keep to this ambling pace, but certainly was not bred for hard or swift riding. To one of his position, the dregs of the stable were considered proper. To ride at all seemed strange—he was far more used to travel by foot, slipping through woodlands where a horse might not easily find any road at all.

This was not to be a hunt today—more an outing for the countess. Though, if they managed to start an osbuck once they were on the hill track, there was no reason not to avail themselves of the opportunity for getting fresh meat. Hans Holdfast had even added a pack pony to their party in hopes of just such luck.

But it was Gregor Knapper who moved up beside Rhys now, that ever-taunting grin crooking his lips.

"Prepared for the Loden, youngling?" His eyes flitted from Rhys' bow and quiver to the short hunter's sword in his belt sheath. "I'll wager that the creature would be shaking in all his scales—like enough to shake them off his body—could he just see the mighty hunter Rhys on the trail."

Rhys had learned patience with such as Gregor long ago. He knew he was slight of body, younger than his years in the eyes of a man like Gregor, who won last Harvest Days' wrestling matches. Best let the fellow mouth his jibes and not give him a chance to see that he was in any way striking home.

Which he was not. The Loden? That was a spook story for children—a mountain legend so well worn by years of telling and retelling that it could no longer ruffle any wayfarer. If there ever had been such a creature—and he did not deny that some odd things had been known to exist in the mountains in the days before men had pushed very far into their somber heights—it was long since gone.

He raised a grin.

"Would my lord earl give a good bounty for such?" he asked. "Fill a purse tight enough and he'll have half the valley out sniffing trails. What about you, Gregor? You gave Jock his three falls in wrestling, can you do the same for the Loden, perhaps?"

Gregor spat as if the dust from the road tickled his throat and filled his mouth.

"There may be worse than the Loden up there." He nodded toward the heights beyond.

Rhys straightened a little in the saddle. "Wolfheads? There's been no sign of such this half year or more."

"Yes, and you can swear to that with your sniffing woods ranging, youngling. But the earl, he has himself a good collection of unfriends here and there, and it might move one or two of them someday to stir up a broth of trouble—"

"Ha, Gregor!" That summons had come from one of the guard and the man urged his horse forward in answer. Rhys was left to share the rearguard, if one might call it such, with Forken, who was leading the donkey and moaning a little to himself now and then, having paid too good attention last night to the ale. He was not an inspiring trail companion, and Rhys' interest turned instead to the scene immediately around him. They were coming out of the lane where it ran through the upper meadows, in which sheep and goats were already grazing, into the fringe of the woods which ran on up to the tangled great forests above.

However, hereabouts the wood was tamed. Fallen tree branches had been rigorously gathered for firewood during the winter—the earl allowed all the farmers fair shares in such a gleaning. He was a good lord and his people fared well.

There were spring flowers showing pink and white and blue-violet among the leaves. Here and there a squirrel sat on a branch overhead, chattering impudently at them as they passed beneath his perch.

On they traveled at a sober pace, twice stopping so that the countess could see some spread of flowers, and once so that she was able to drink water from a spring and remark that it was nearly as sweet as wine, so clear it ran.

Now the wood thickened. Rhys moved uneasily in his saddle. He was too used to being afoot, ranging out into the trees and brush which fenced the trail. Something—he shook his head off as if to warn off some buzzing fly—something was amiss.

All his life he had had queer starts, but had known from an early age that they must not be spoken of among his fellows. A man could have some skill of weapon or strength of body, but a strange pricking of an inner talent was not accepted.

He wanted to urge his mount ahead, even to call out to Captain Karvan of the guard. The further they rode, the more the uneasiness gripped him. At last he could stand it no longer. He unslung his bow and strung it.

"What'd see?" Froken's bleary eyes turned in his direction. "Master Loren ain't given any order t' hunt."

"Just testing," Rhys made quick answer. He could not shoot well from the saddle after all, even if a quadbear was to rear up before him.

Only it was no quadbear and there were others who could shoot, truly and deadly, from among the greenery. Rhys jerked and dropped his bow as a shaft skewered his upper arm. At the same time, his horse gave a shrill cry of pain and stamped on into those ahead with a second shaft, near feather deep, in its side. It stumbled and went to its knees, and Rhys had just time to swing off, stumbling forward, fumbling for the hilt of his ranger's sword.

The narrow wooded road was all wild confusion. Mounts were down kicking and men lay still or screamed. There was a swirl of riders around the countess, her guards closed tightly about her—but to no purpose. There was no one in sight to fight, only the arrows which continued to pick them off.

As he made his way toward that embattled knot, Rhys wondered about the attack. No battle cries sounded except those of Vars. Who had sprung this vicious ambush and why?

He caught his foot in a tangle of rein from one of the downed horses and fell forward, his head cracking against the saddle of another felled beast. There was a flash of pain so intense it whirled him away as he collapsed to the ground. A moment later, one of the defenders of the countess fell across his inert body, great gouts of blood covering them both.

2

Sarita, having carefully wound the last curling thread end on the spool, sat for a moment, wriggling her fingers to loosen the cramp caused by such concentrated fine work. It must be past noon-ing—time for her to go down to the buttery for her ration of bread, cheese, and mild ale. She was hungry, she realized suddenly.

There were no longer any sounds from the nursery, which shared this level of the tower. Perhaps Halda had taken her charge out for an airing.

Sarita got up—and froze. From outside the window came a wild clamor. Over her head thundered the great alarm bell, which she had never heard put to use before. The violence of its clanging seem to shake the very walls about her. Eerie shouts from below the window drew her.

She could see the great gate from there, and it had been pushed ajar. Not for the return of the party that had ridden forth this morn-ing, but for a rabble of running, screaming women hauling children by the hand or carrying babies, and men with pitchforks or threshing flails in their hands, the few weapons of the field workers.

They stormed into the courtyard, and Sarita saw three of the guards strain to shut the gate behind them before the great bar dropped into place. Var-The-Outer was no great castle, fortified as one of the keeps nearer the rich bottom lands. There had been no raids of wolfheads heard of here for years—except some skirmishes in winter—well beyond the walls between the ill-armed outlaws and guards or rangers. Certainly no such band of half-starved and ill-weaponed men had started this rout!

She strained to see the small village. There was smoke—and distant screams so thin and far away that her ears barely caught the sound.

There called now, after the alarm bell had given its last thunderous clang, the whistle of the guard sergeants. But half their number had ridden out that morning. . . . The women and children from the village had been pushed and shoved into cover—they must now be in the great hall, while those able to bear arms—some of the grooms and even the cook's boy (he flourished an iron spit nearly as tall as himself)—came out and were shouted and cuffed into forming a defense line of sorts.

Those bowmen left were already on the heights. Sarita had heard the race of feet on the stairs outside her own chamber as some must have gone to the crown of the tower.

Yet, save for that dark curl of smoke from the village, nothing moved in the open near the keep. Sarita's hands crooked again. Weapon work was beyond any learning she had. But—

She drew away from the window to stare about her at the two standing frames with half-finished work stretched across them, at the bare walls and the herb and rush-strewn floor underfoot. The keep was well set and Earl Florian had over the years seen to its constant maintenance. How could outlaws think of storming it?

Were they wolfheads? Rumors she had only half heard came to mind. Earl Florian had been the principal regent for the young High King. He had held straightly to the laws, endeavoring to turn over to his young master a strong and rich kingdom when the day came. And so—being the man he was—he had made enemies. There were several lords who had been prevented from private wars with their neighbors. He had stood up to the town guilds and saw to a fair taxing system.

And, if they could not attack the earl in his might, they could well try to achieve their purpose by seizing the countess or little Lord Valoris!

There had been no war in Sarita's lifetime, but she had heard enough from the talk of veterans who had taken their ease by the winter fires, and from such as Marva, poor wench!

Marva was from the north. She had been a serf-slave until the earl, who would have none such serve him, had freed her. A proper washerwoman she was now—but once she had been something much greater. Sometimes she had evil dreams and awoke the whole of the maids' sleeping chamber with her cries. When they roused her, she blurted out horrible things and then stopped in midword to weep and rock herself back and forth on her bed, until old Gressa could soothe her to sleep again.

It would take an army to overrun Var-The-Outer, Sarita tried to reassure herself. How could an army have come into this land without being detected by the rangers who kept boundary watch? Still she began a search of the room—just why, she could not tell.

The outer walls holding the window were stone, but the two inner ones were paneled with fancifully carved dark wood. In one was the door leading to the stair; in the other there was no break, and she knew that Halda's domain was behind that.

There was no bar for the door, only a simple latch such as fastened any inner keep portal. As for furniture, beside the frames and a long table for measuring and cutting, there were only the stools on which she and her mistress sat to work.

Measuring and cutting— Her hand went to the straps on her belt. Her scissors hung there, their blades honed as sharp as any sword blade within these walls. She had the packet of needles, never letting them far from her—needles were too precious not to be guarded as another guildsman would guard his strong box. And lying on the table was the great measure. It was as long as her arm, a piece of wood aged and heavy enough to hold the cloth to be cut in place without a wrinkle.

She was about to go and pick it up when there was another burst of sound from without. Sarita once more pulled herself up for a full view from the window, looking at what was advancing over the fields.

They wore the ragged and rusty garments and ringed leather shirts of masterless men. Still, they rode in a wide order so that the archers—if there were any skillful and strong enough to bring down his man at such a distance—could take them only one at a time. Behind this skirmish line were knots of riders, and among them Sarita caught sight of a flutter of green. The countess—plainly she must be a prisoner.

One of the knot raised a hand in a signal and his men drew to either side to reveal their captive, held in a vise grip by a man behind her in the saddle. Her hunting cap was gone and her loose hair fell about her shoulders. Her face was white and set, though a red bruise blemished the lower part of her face and a trickle of blood runneled from the corner of her mouth.

Against her throat rested the edge of a knife, and it was plain that he who held it could use it as he willed.

There was a sudden silence. Those on the walls watched with strained eyes as the invaders moved leisurely onward, coming to a halt within hailing distance of the walls.

"Open gate!" the voice arose, whether from the man who held the countess or one of his followers, Sarita could not tell. "Open gate, scum, or we open throat!"

A good archer—would one dare to try to take out the man who held the countess? Sarita knew little of bow work. But the invader's message was plain: a single stroke and their lady would be dead.

There was a milling below, and an argument which was finally shouted down by the senior sergeant. Sarita saw men trail to either side, leaving a path. The sergeant stepped to the gate bar and pulled on it; two of his men helped him pull the ponderous barrier open.

Then there was a wild rush. Those men who had ridden at such a leisurely pace spurred on their mounts and thundered in, lashing down at the unmounted defenders.

"No quarter!"

Sarita saw the countess topple limply from her horse, spattered with blood, tossed aside like a broken branch. There were screams from the courtyard.

Sarita never knew how the measuring rod had come into her hands, but it was there. From that one cry she knew that there would be little hope. She could only wish to die rather than live to become like Marva, a broken, haunted thing.

The latch at the door jiggled—surely they had not gotten up so far yet? She picked up her stool with her other hand, ready to hurl it. However, when the door flew open a body crashed to the floor and she heard the angry screams of the child Halda had brought with her. From between the old nurse's thin shoulders protruded the hilt of a knife.

Sarita sprang forward, dragging Halda further in and pulling the red-faced, screaming child with her. She slammed the door and, with all her strength, pushed one of the heavy frames against it. Small enough defense, but all she had.

Halda was not dead. She had lifted herself a little, her hands braced against the floor. Sarita crouched beside her, and the woman's eyes seemed to burn into hers.

"May the Hell of Beman the Thrice-Damned—"

A flood of blood stiffled her words. She shook her head and spat a great gout.

"Janine—that traitorous slut! Listen—they had their spy here right enough, but they did not get the young master!" There was determination in her harsh voice. "Nor will they. Listen to me, girl! Help me up."

With Sarita's assistance she arose to a sitting position, one shoulder braced against the edge of the frame that blocked the door. There was a bundle of cloth fast in her apron. Sarita recognized it as the back sling to carry the child. When the girl would have reached for the knife hilt in the nurse's back, Halda's hand caught hers with a firmer grip than the girl would have thought possible.

"Leave it—draw it and I die—fast—there is that to be done."

Valoris crouched at Halda's side, one small, bloodstained hand fast in the fold of her skirt. His small body was shaking.

"They want the young lordling—to use to torment our lord. They will—not—get—him—" The nurse was faltering now, drawing short breaths, spitting out blood between each word.

"Belt—" Her hand moved in the shortest of gestures. "Give him sweetie—he will—will be—easy—for you then—it will last a day. Do it!"

Sarita found the belt pouch about Halda's waist and brought out a sticky ball wrapped in a leaf.

She held it out and the child grabbed at it, sticking it in his mouth.

"The wall—there—" Halda's hand had lifted to lie on Valoris' small head.

"Press head—eagle and fox—together!" Blood once more came in a flood as Sarita followed orders. There was a sliding of the wall and she was looking into a very narrow stair leading downward.

Halda fumbled with the back sling—tossed it weakly in Sarita's direction.

"Take—take—him—and go—now!"

There was certainly noise closer to hand. Sarita shrugged on the back sling and somehow caught up the child to be stowed within. She also took up the measure again: the hole was dark and would be darker when this door was closed—she needed something to feel the way ahead.

The child was quiet enough now, but his weight pulled at her shoulders. Behind her the door swung firmly shut, sealing them in.

Pain was red and hot. Rhys tried to shift under the burden which had pinned him to the ground. He could smell the stink of blood and horse and, above all, death. The ambush!

As memory returned he again tried to move, only to be stopped by words which came from close by.

"My lord wants no prisoners. Except this little bird we've caught—she's our key to the keep. They are all dead—but look you—no looting—leave that for our friends up mountain. We promised them that much for showing us the back way in. You, Simeon, and Jock—be sure no one is alive, and then tell our mountain friends that they can come in—the mangy scum will be only too glad to have the sword work done for them."

Then he heard hooves moving away. Rhys understood—they had the countess! But outlaws had never been known to set up such a well-arranged ambush. If not wolfheads—then who?

He tried to lift his head and then thought better of it. There might just be a chance that if he continued to lie half-covered this way, he could be considered one of the dead. Better not risk a slit throat—he had his own score to settle now, and it was a deep one.

Instead, he lay listening. Once he heard a groan and then a muffled cry. So one of his company had survived—until now. The weight on him was rolled off. He tried to hold his breath. He was lying facedown, and that heavy smell of blood, the wetness about his head and shoulders, suggested the one who had fallen over him had drenched him. Hopefully it would be enough to mask that he was still alive.

It was the hardest thing he had ever done in his life to lie and wait—wait to be rolled over, to see as his last sight on earth a knife plunge down into his throat. But that did not come; apparently he was so ghastly a sight that they assumed he was dead.

He heard comments and tried from what little they said to get some idea of their identity—whose liegemen they were. By now he had firmly decided that they were disciplined and well-trained troopers.

At last he heard the snorting of a horse and one of the men shout out:

"Get them back, you fool, blood scent will send them wild!"

Again he felt the ground under him tremble to the beat of hooves. Yet he continued to lie still. He had a pounding headache, which nearly blinded him with its force, and the arrow wound in his arm was another raging torment. He felt his stomach churn, set awry by the odors about him.

Rhys was not even sure he had strength enough to crawl. At last he levered his hands under him and forced himself up so that he was sitting in the midst of the dead—both men and horses.

His bow was gone, but his hunter's sword lay in the bloody mud and he retrieved it from where he sat. The words of the devil who had planned all this came back to his mind—these enemies had made some kind of deal with the mountain outlaws. They were to have the picking of the field—which meant arms, even clothing. And they would be no more willing to aid him than the men who had killed all the friends and companions he knew.

He rose to his knees and was immediately sick, his body wrenched with the force of his heaving. Oddly enough, that seemed to clear his head somewhat.

A bow—he had lost his bow. Now he forced himself to look around and finally staggered to where Gregor lay, his bristly chin pointing to the sky and his blue eyes staring.

"Need it—will pay blood price, comrade." Rhys choked out the words as he took Gregor's weapon. Having that, he was emboldened to take up a sword which lay some distance away, as if its despairing owner had hurled it from him. With swords and bow in hand, he made for that same screen of brush from behind which death had come.

3

Thank the Great Lady it was not altogether dark ahead and Sarita, once her eyes adjusted to the gloom, could catch wan gleams of light from below. At least the child was giving her no trouble. His breath against her cheek carried a scent she half-remembered. When she had that monstrous toothache a few months ago, the old nurse had given her something to rub on her gum which had not only banished the pain but made her drowsy for half the morning.

With Valoris' weight sagging against her back, she descended one step at a time. When she reached the first source of light, she saw that it was a mere crack between the stones of the wall.

There was fresher air there, but she could also hear the others again, and the screams led her imagination to paint the full horror of what must be happening within the keep. That shout of "No quarter!" struck home, and she leaned a shoulder against the wall, limp with terror. Who had done this thing—and why? Halda had appeared to have known something—had she not spoken of Janine the nursery maid as a traitoress?

Valoris nuzzled against her, his sticky lips against her cheek. Yes, the child! Though *she* had sworn no liege oath to the earl, who would let a child fall into the bloody hands of those now busy about their deadly business?

A coal of anger flared under her fear. Earl Florian had been a good lord and just. And his lady—she had been all that was kind and merciful. Sarita's free hand clenched on the measuring rod as though it were the haft of a spear.

15

Halda must have known there was a measure of safety at the end of this hidden way—now was the time to prove the nurse right. She still went with care past two more of the wall slits. Though she could not truly judge, she believed that she was now level with the courtyard. Ahead was deep darkness with no promise of any more ghostly fingers of light.

Sarita shifted the child and again leaned against the cold dankness of the wall for a breathing space. She wished for a moment that the little lordling was *not* the hale and healthy weight that he was.

However, she could not remain where she was. How could she be sure that this secret way might not be sniffed out—though she knew that Halda would have done all she could do to conceal it. By using the rod as a cane, she discovered that the steps were widening out, giving her more foot room.

There was a dampish smell of slimed stone and seldom-stirred air about her now. Still Sarita pressed forward, her hope of escape feeding the anger rising in her.

Though she was town-bred and knew little of the countryside, she felt they would have more of a chance were she to reach the open. The rod clicked and pushed forward a little at the same level; she must have reached the foot of the stairway.

However, the passage was no wider here; in fact, it seemed to close in upon her. Twice her rod told her of a narrower space and she had to turn sidewise, holding the straps of the sling as tightly as she could so that Valoris would not be scraped from her back.

How long she walked, Sarita never knew. It seemed to her that she had been at least a full spin of the sandclock trapped in this musty dark. Valoris whimpered once or twice, but then she was sure he must be sleepy. She ached under his weight, but she dared not pause or try to lay him down—not on the surface underfoot, from which strong and nasty odors arose.

Again there was a glimmer of light ahead, and in spite of her fatigue Sarita hurried toward it. It was as thin and gray as that of the window slits, but it was enough to show her that the passage had ended in a cramped space as wide as a cupboard room. The walls were solid bedrock except the one directly facing her, where

the slit was cut beside another dark opening, perhaps a further passage.

For the moment Sarita could go no farther. She dropped the rod, which clattered painfully against her foot, and twisted off her long work apron, loosening it awkwardly with one hand. Once that fell to the floor, she lowered the child onto it and squatted on her heels beside him, breathing heavily.

Hunger and thirst—she pushed aside the needs of her body. There certainly was no bread, cheese, or ale to be served up here. After a long moment or two she stood up again, trying to see something through the slit. But it certainly was no window for viewing, and all she could distinguish was that outside somewhere it must still be day.

At length she gathered up Valoris, wrapped in the apron around the back sling, and made resolutely for the passage on the other side of the light slit. This whole maze had been made for a purpose, and Sarita was sure that it had been intended as a bolthole for just such a circumstance as she now found herself in.

Once more she put the rod into play, feeling out the way ahead. For a short time, perhaps twenty steps, her soft leather shoes met the harshness of stone blocks. Then, abruptly, she was walking on earth—earth which smelled sour. There was an odd wavering of light farther on that came, she discovered when she reached it, from a scattering of spongy growths rising from the floor to knee level, clinging to the walls.

There was a skittering and Sarita froze. Something small, moving so fast she could not see it properly, flashed from one mound of growth to the next. So this place had more than one sort of life. And none of it such as she wanted to examine more closely.

Yet the fungi-grown way stretched on and on. Sarita's head ached and she began to fear that the air here was polluted with some poisonous fumes which would sap her strength. She set her teeth and trudged ahead.

Her reckoning might be all wrong, but she believed that she was now beyond the keep walls. When would this cursed way come to an end?

It came when her measure struck against stone once more. Again there were steps, this time leading upward. She sank down on them, too exhausted to go any further at the moment. The child whimpered again. One of his arms was about her neck. She had none of Halda's skills for child caring. Her best might not be enough to even keep him alive. Sarita tried to fight such thoughts away.

Sarita had never done much more in weekly meetings of the chapel than listen to the exhortion of the priestess, obediently read her praise book, and bring altar flowers on feast days. The Great Lady had no fervent follower in her. She wet her lips now with a dry tongue and wondered dimly about prayer, but what she had seen this day had made her believe that the Dark had been more powerful than the Light.

With a weary sigh she somehow began what was nearly a crawl up the flight of stairs. There were no more of the ghostly light fungi here, and she believed that she could feel the darkness as if a curtain or web from one of her own work frames wreathed her round.

Once more she reached a level space and there was light— more than she had seen since she had entered this way; enough to make her eyes blink. She could plainly distinguish rubble piled up high, as if some wall had collapsed, leaving only the lit space at the top to suggest that beyond lay freedom.

Sarita settled the child on the floor and gingerly hunted a way up that barrier which would not bring it rattling down upon her. At length her body lay along the bruising stones at the top and she was looking out.

It was not sunlight beyond, rather the beginning of dusk. That was a piece of luck. She strained to see as much as she could. There were trees about. Had she come under the meadows around the keep far enough to reach the forested knolls? That thought heartened her.

While she still had some light it might be well to shift what stones she could to give her easier passage—she would need far more room carrying Valoris. Slowly, her arms and back aching, Sarita set to work.

The brush that had screened the attackers was rent enough in places by their mounts, that Rhys found passage easily enough. He put several layers of brush between him and the road before he wavered to a tree and set his back to it, dropping bow and longsword at his feet (he had set his own blade back in its belt sheath) to examine his arm.

His fall had snapped off the shaft, and he felt the head well out of the flesh it had penetrated. Setting his teeth and cringing, he put all the strength he could summon into a sudden pull. There was a blaze of pain so great that he reeled and crumpled to the ground, darkness closing in upon him once more.

It was moisture on his face which wakened him. The fairness of the spring day had given way with the approaching dusk to a steady rain. Time—even as he opened his mouth to the rain, the thought of time struck him. Had the mountain wolfheads come a-plundering? If they had, why was he still alive? Such fortune was rarely given any man.

His arm burned with pain and a new fear nibbled at his resolution. Untreated wounds had their own way of killing, and it was not an easy one. Yet he was sure he dared not venture toward Var-The-Outer for any aid. If the keep had had warning, they would be locked tight and between those walls and him would range the very ones who had sent that arrow flying.

No, he must find some place to lie up until he could do more than stagger around. There were plants every ranger knew which could both relieve his pain and reduce infection. Once truly able to keep his feet, he would turn to use his scouting skills to find out just what had struck so viciously at his world—who and why.

Somehow he won to his feet. The wolfheads certainly had learned plenty of wilderness tricks during their mountain lives. Would they be ready to find any signs of one who had survived the massacre?

He leaned back against the tree. The dusk was thickening now and sometimes things looked hazy, as if there were a veil between his eyes and what lay about. But he must find a refuge, if only for the night.

Rhys was familiar with the road they had taken west. It was the common way for hunters and a handful of traders who brought furs down in the spring. He was now to the south of that road. He closed his eyes and tried to recall old landmarks—so well known to him that they could have been of his own setting.

South—yes! There was the logging boundary! Just this past season the earl had given orders that a section of southland be logged out so the grazing land be increased. Asher's Wood had been chosen, for it had been burnt over four years past and most of the large trees killed, the small ones left but charred sticks. They had cut down what was left of the dead oaks and dragged the logs to a pile to be drawn on later when the wood was seasoned.

He lurched away from the tree support, bow and sword again in hand, though he was inwardly certain that he could not use either were some foe to rise out of the gathering dark in challenge. However, he was heartened by catching sight of one of the boundary marker stones and knew that he was heading toward his hoped-for shelter. Luckily he had been one of those overseeing the cutting so that good growing timber not be harmed. It had been his first real test for that part of his ranger-huntsman's job.

Rhys tried hard to use hunter's silence in passage, but such skill was beyond him now. He could only stop at intervals and listen for any sound of the night that was not native here. Once a great owl swept from a tree as he passed, and a second or so later he heard the death cry of its prey.

There were no predators this close to the keep—other than those two-legged ones who had come to ravage today. Had he been higher in the mountains, he would have been easy taking for a quadbear or one of the pards that hunted from the snowline down. This wood was fairly tame.

Luckily, here under the trees he was not buffeted by the worst of the storm, but somewhere he heard the thunderous crash of an age-old tree brought down by some fierce wind current. Most creatures would keep under cover tonight.

How far was he from his goal? Rhys stopped and thrust the sword through his belt, tried to rub his hand across his forehead, only to awaken a worse throb as his hand touched a well-raised bump. He was rapidly tiring and did not know how long he could keep on.

Then the whole world flared with light and he realized that he was at the very edge of the woods with lightning playing in the sky overhead.

Now he must locate the log pile. Was he east or west of it? A gust of rain struck him full in the face as he pushed through the bushes which had grown since the logging.

There was another flash of eye-searing light from the skies, enough to blind him for a moment or two. These spring storms were often so destructive as to kill any beast caught in the fields.

Trees could attract lightning: this burned-over stretch before him was evidence of that. He must move out into the open even though he was drenched by rain, buffeted cruelly by the storm winds until he could hardly keep his feet.

He was so storm-lost that he was not aware he had found what he sought until he ran full into the knee-high barrier of a log. He spralled across it, yet hardly cared as weariness overtook him and he fell fast asleep in the drenching rain.

4

A storm was breaking outside. Sarita edged back on her precarious perch as cold rain and wind thrust at her. She had been well on the way to breaking past the barrier when this had struck. To venture out into that continually rising fury with no protection and with Valoris was something she could not bring herself to dare.

There was a tremendous bolt of lightning, the glare of which reached her. Sarita edged down and drew the child into her arms.

Valoris whimpered and then cried, not with the full force of his lungs, but rather like some small frightened animal. She held him close and somehow remembered a song she had heard Halda croon:

> "Little lamb, thy dame is near.
> There is naught for you to fear.
> The dark has come but it will go,
> Sun will come, Great Mother wishes so."

The dank chill of this place was seeping into them both. Sarita began rocking back and forth, singing the words over and over. The child whimpered again. His arms wrapped around her neck and he buried his face against her shoulder.

"Little lamb—" And that he was—no more able to fend for himself than any of the newborn bundles of white wool and spindly legs that she had seen in the early spring.

"Thy dame is near—" Resolutely she fought memory—the memory of that slender body and its green cloak thrown aside as one would throw a useless rag.

23

Were some of the old tales true—could the dead who died with a concern for the living (and Sarita was sure that was what the Countess Wanda had done) remain somehow in spirit to give what aid they could?

There was the Lady—when she had come to a woman's estate, she had spent her night's vigil in the small chapel in the great cathedral, the Great Fane, at Raganfors. Any woman seeking comfort was welcome there, for the Lady held fast a large portion of the Great Power as her own: the power of quickening life, of fruitfulness, of love of child and hearthside.

As the girl continued to sing, Sarita tried to remember the embroidered picture of the Lady in her cloak, which had hung behind the altar. At the time of her vigil she had been in wonder at the perfect work of the artisans who had wrought it more so than of what it represented. She had been so immersed then in her desire to be one of the great artists, to be able to make at least a shadow of such as she saw.

Now—the Lady. Though her lips shaped the words of her song in her mind, others came clearly:

"Lady—spread wide your cloak over us."

Valoris had stopped whimpering. She could hope that he was asleep. Her whole body ached. She wanted nothing more than to lie down and sleep—to forget all of this day of horror, this night of storm.

Moving very cautiously, she edged down a little until she was nearly supine. She slept, the child resting against her shoulder.

His crying brought her out of jumbled dreams of which she could remember nothing. He had squirmed out of her hold and was slapping at her face. She could see him clearly, for there was light coming through the hole she had tried to widen last night and it was clear and bright. The wrath of the storm had swept by.

"Hungry—breadies—breadies—now!"

Valoris' face was growing redder. Whatever had been in that sweet treat to keep him quiet had worn off now.

Hungry, of course he must be hungry! That thought awakened her own inner gnawing. But they must get out of here to find any food—if they could at all. She attempted to push the thought out of her mind.

"Valoris, wait here." She pulled away from his hold. She was not really sure, in spite of all the tales of how forward and knowing he was, just how much he could understand. She could only hope that he would. She pointed up to where she had been working the night before. "Make hole bigger, go through—"

He stared upward at the band of light. "Want Hally, want Hally now!"

"Halda can't come here." Sarita tried valiantly to find some answer he would understand. "We go—"

"Go Hally! Hally have breadies—go Hally now!"

At least he probably would not resist her until she got him out of this hole. She must take one small step at a time and concentrate on that.

Somehow she managed to pull herself up the treacherous rubble and worm her way out, then turn to draw the child after her.

They were, she could see now, in a circle of trees, and the sun was well up. Evidences of the storm were present in torn leaves upon the ground and thick water drops which still rained on their heads from branches above.

"Hally—" Valoris' small face twisted. "Want Hally— breadies—"

It would seem that only a lie would serve. She bent her aching back and swung the child up against her. Food—where could she find any food in this wilderness? To try to head back toward any of the farms was to walk straight into the hands of the hunters.

"We go Hally," she said, and wavered on, steadying herself now and then against the trunk of one tree or another, not sure in what direction she was heading or what in the way of help could be offered here.

Valoris began to cry with full-lunged anger, and she tried to keep one hand over his mouth as he struggled to get down and beat at her with his small fists. Would those who had taken Var-The-Outer be searching these woods for any fugitives?

He bit her hand sharply enough to make her lose her hold, then he let out one piercing scream of pure temper. Sarita looked about wildly. What could she do?

Then—could it really be that they were indeed sheltered under the Lady's cloak she had seen spread in the chapel years back?—

she sighted a patch of new green growth near one of the trees. Though she knew little of herb craft, there were some plants used so commonly that any woman would know them upon sight.

With Valoris kicking in her grasp, she went to her knees and tugged at a bunch of green, the strength of her pull bringing it out of the ground roots and all.

Seally leaf—it made excellent salads and children who went Maying in the fields and woods always came back with their lips stained green by it. It was sweet to the taste and was an acceptable food—especially in the spring.

"Eat!" Perhaps the sharp note in her voice checked him as he opened his mouth for another yell. Into the open mouth Sarita pushed a small wad of leaves.

Surprised, he gummed it, angry tears still on his cheeks. She loosed her hold on him a little, enough to take up a mouthful herself. There was a fresh and sweet taste to this woodland bounty, and she chewed eagerly. Valoris had some teeth—whether to masticate this, she was not sure. But he did not seem to be in any trouble. She saw him swallow and his small hand come out to grab for more.

There was a rustling in the bushes at one side and scarlet feathers not to be mistaken flashed across where they crouched, swooping at them. Valoris gave a small cry and grabbed upward for the bird circling them, giving voice loudly.

Sarita looked speculatively at the bush. A nesting bird warning off intruders? A nest might mean eggs. She dragged tighter the sling she had left around the child, then knotted that to the measuring rod, which she hammered into the ground as an anchor. Hoping her charge was secure, she forced her way into the bush and found the nest right enough: four brown-shelled eggs. She could not be sure how fresh they were, but being finicky over food was for the past.

She took two of the eggs—great as her need might be she would hold to the teaching of the Lady. Once out in the open she sat down beside Valoris. His face was grimy with earth from the leaves of the plant, but he was still busy pulling off bits for himself now, cramming them into his mouth.

Sarita unlatched her scissors from her girdle and with infinite care she pecked a hole in the top of the eggshell and sniffed. Fresh-laid it must be. Gingerly she picked away minute bits of the top of the shell and held it to Valoris lips.

"In!" she ordered, and tipped the shell. Its contents popped into the child's mouth, open in pure astonishment. He made a face as if to spit it out again, but she held his mouth firmly closed until he swallowed, though she feared to lose the other egg in a struggle before she could eat it herself.

They needed water. The rain on the plant leaves and the moisture of the eggs had given them some relief, but she knew that she must soon find true water. Water could also mean other things: watercress, if such grew hereabouts, and perhaps fish, though the catching and preparation of those was a problem.

Untethering Valoris, she gathered him up and looked around. In which direction? She could wander, helplessly lost in this wood — which for all she knew might spread on to join the great forest — or come out abruptly in the open.

Drawing a deep breath Sarita closed her eyes and made another silent petition to the Lady. Then opening them again, she walked steadily forward — though in a zigzag line, as she avoided trees and brush too thick for her to fight her way through.

It was because of such a stand of brush, when she avoided it, that she discovered curtained traces of an old road, little deeper than a farm track, but the first evidence she had seen that her own kind had ever come this way.

The rain had puddled in its deep ruts and there were no signs, judging by her very small knowledge, of any recent hoofprints. A road must lead somewhere, and she decided that it would be her guide.

Sun touched into the crevice between two logs, one of which had rolled from its top site on a large pile. It centered to warm the body which lay limply in that rough bed.

Rhys felt the warmth dimly and opened his eyes to the glare of full day. He tried to sit up and his first, too quick, movement brought a cry out of him as his injured arm brushed against one of the charred sides of his temporary shelter.

His clothing was sodden. He raised his good arm to take his sleeve into his mouth and suck. The moisture seemed to clear his head, little as it was. He made another try at getting up, this time steadying himself against the big log. Then he staggered back until his shoulders thumped against the pile of wood and brought another groan out of him.

At least he had made his goal through the storm. This was the burnt and cleared strip of forest where he had worked the past summer in charge of the crew of farmboys who had felled what was left of the trees. There was green showing now here and there, spring growth refreshed and renewed by the rain.

Water— He shook his aching head slowly and then wished that he had not, for that brought a new flash of pain. Memory had provided him with recall of a spring not too far away. They had used it while they had labored here.

Slowly he worked his way from between the tree trunks that had been his shelter and lurched out into the open. His bow was strapped to his shoulder; the sword he had thrust through his belt the night before was a weight now, dragging at him, but he had no intention of losing it. Instead he wavered from one careful step to the next, making for the spring. It was a fair day, as if there had never been such a wracking storm. Whether he had wolfheads on his trail now, he did not know. In his present state he was certainly in no condition to stand to arms. Concentrate on one thing at a time—that was all he could do now.

He saw the brilliant green of the new growth about the spring. A leaper arose on its thick hind legs, looked wide-eyed at him, and took off with one of those amazing jumps they could show upon occasion. Rhys watched its flight with regret. Food— But with his arm so injured he could not put string to his salvaged bow, much less let an arrow fly.

At last he allowed himself to fall full length in tangled grass to drink by dipping his chin into the small pool fed by the spring.

The water on his face seemed to ease the throbbing of his head a little and he stuck his whole head below its surface for the space of a breath, rising with his hair plastered and dripping in runnels onto the scuffed leather of his sleeveless jerkin as he looked about him with clearer wits than he had known since his wakening.

As he came to his knees, his belt pouch caught on the sword, reminding him of its presence. His ranger's pouch— Opening it, he removed the herb-soaked moss that every ranger carried as a medicinal for animal or human, and quickly made it into a poultice, which he secured onto his injured arm by pulling the sleeve back down. That accomplished, he sat back on his heels to think.

Was there any way of reaching Var-The-Outer? He was somehow sure that those who had laid the ambush were between him and the keep. He remembered what they had said of the countess— that she was to be their key. Yes, with no man there who could stand the ill usage of their well-loved mistress, those killers could put that key to use quickly enough. They certainly would have also swept the village and perhaps by now all of the valley farms. He was surely on his own and must make his own way.

But to where? To Raganfors to report this disaster to the earl? There were ways in plenty of keeping him from ever getting that far. The pass must already be enemy-held, the wolfheads aroused to be on watch for just such a messenger.

No, he had to wait until he was fit, until he could learn just what had happened—and, most of all, who was the enemy.

Suddenly his turmoil of thought was broken. That was crying he heard! A child—certainly no animal. Survivors from the valley?

Rhys edged up from his place by the spring, but he did not move forward yet. That well-laid ambush remained in his mind— could the enemy have the brazen cruelty to use a frightened child to draw out of hiding any who had fled? He snarled and worked his way behind the rock encasement of the spring. Setting his wounded arm in the front of his jerkin for support, he used his other hand to lift the sword.

He waited, sure that sound was now advancing toward him, down the rough track which the loggers had made.

5

The ruts on the road were so deep and filled with storm water that Sarita tried to keep to the verge for more level footing. She was also fighting Valoris, who was screaming now in full rage and twisting perilously in the sling, kicking until she nearly dropped him.

"Want Hally—hungry—" he got out between screams, and hit her with his fists. Flinching, Sarita staggered back and, unable to keep her balance, landed in the thick mud of the road with force enough to bring a grunt out of her.

The sling had slipped and the child, after another yell, was on his hands and knees scuttling away from her into the middle of the one-time road, mud splashing up about him, plastering his small body.

Sarita's aching arms had flopped to either side of her body and for a long moment she made no attempt to move. It was as if this last mishap had drained the remnants of strength which had kept her going for so long. Though she was not aware of it, tears of frustration runneled through the mud splatters on her own face. Her loosened hair clung damply about her.

Valoris' defiant escape had not taken him far. He was squatting in a nearby mud pool, his attention apparently distracted for the moment as he scooped up the wet clay and threw it about.

Now as she slid over to his side, she was aware of something else, an odor. The child had soiled himself and could not be left so. If she could only find water other than these mud puddles . . .

The mess of leaves and egg had certainly not filled his stomach successfully, and now he was trying a new experiment. Opening his mouth, the boy was about to push a fistful of the mud into it. Sarita did not even try to get to her feet. Reaching over, she slapped down his hand before it quite reached Valoris' lips.

He flailed back at her and screamed again, but she caught both his hands and held them.

At that moment she wanted to fling back her unkempt head and wail as loudly as Valoris. She had none of the talents of a nursemaid and certainly she could not conjure fresh clothes or the right kind of food out of thin air.

Valoris was fighting her hold, his face turning red with anger, his eyes squeezed shut. Now he tried to kick at her with first one foot and then the other.

"Where are you from?" Those words, which cut through the child's screams, came as a shock.

Though she did not loosen her hold on Valoris, Sarita jerked halfway around. There was indeed someone standing there, a bared sword in one hand, the other tucked into the front of his jerkin.

Under mud she recognized the dark green livery of the rangers. When she looked closely into the drawn face, a grayish cast under its weathered brown, she knew the man also. This was the youngest of the rangers—what was his name?—Roose—no *Rhys*, Rhys Forgarson. She had heard two of the bower maids discuss him and whether he might be a fit partner for the midsummer feast.

She must have said his name aloud, for he nodded, then grimaced as if that gesture had been answered by pain.

"You are—"

"Sarita Magasdaughter, apprentice to Dame Argalas."

"Then—then you are from the keep! What has happened?"

He wavered down the short alone into the road from the verge. Valoris had ceased his crying to watch this newcomer with round eyes.

"They—outlaws—they brought the countess with steel to her throat and the sergeants opened the gate. Halda—Halda was death-struck by one she said was a traitoress—one of the maids. She brought the young lord into the workroom and before she died showed me a secret way out. They—they were killing—"

First her hands and then her whole body began to shake as

memory closed down. Not that she had seen much slaughter from
her secret stair, but she had heard, and she knew enough from the
old tales to imagine far too keenly what had been the fate of Var's
liegemen and women.

"So—" The word came out of him like a hiss. "And this," he
nodded toward the child, "is Lord Valoris?"

She nodded. But she had questions of her own. "What happened—how did they take the countess—these outlaws?"

"Ambush. But these are no wolfheads. They are menie trained.
And if they do not find him," again he nodded to the child, "within
their slaughter net—they will be seeking. They must have made very
sure of the whole valley by now. And the pass will be guarded." He
appeared to be thinking aloud.

"I have no food for him," Sarita broke in starkly. "We have only
eaten seally and each an egg—raw from the nest."

He looked now as if he were not attending to her, rather staring
down the overgrown road.

"We must have water—food!" she said more loudly. Perhaps he
was cross-witted. There was the sign of a great bruise on his forehead
disappearing to hide under his dark hair.

"You say," he turned on Sarita sharply as if he had not heard a
word she had said, "that Halda was dead by a traitor's hand—who?"

"The maid Janine," Sarita answered impatiently. She did not
know what service this battle survivor could give them, but he was
a ranger and so well aware of what could be found in the woods.
As liegeman to the earl, Valoris must be his concern now.

"How many more?" he said slowly. "And who? All the rangers
who I trained with were slain. I do not think we had a double
tongue among us. Therefore—" He made an impatient gesture in
her direction. "Can you bring the young lordling? One-armed as I
am I cannot carry him. There is a spring back there."

The thought of clean water brought her to her feet and she
tugged Valoris out of his puddle, not attempting to use the sling as
she followed at the pace her guide set back into the bushes and
then across a stretch of burnt land to where rocks stood high and
blessed waving of greenery beckoned them on with promise.

She held out palms full of water for Valoris to drink. Rhys had
disappeared, but came back with what looked like a bundle of thick

reeds. Throwing these down beside her, he said, "Strip one of these with your belt knife—give it to him to suck and chew. It is nourishment of a sort, little as it is."

She followed orders after she had washed the child's hands and face. Then as he did suck avidly on the round stem, she took off his filthy clothing. It was warm enough in the patch of the sun to leave him so while she followed the pool down further and there washed the small garments as best she could, returning with the front of her smock dress wet well down the front. Their guide had disappeared for a second time, and she wondered where with a growing uneasiness. She knew he was no outlaw, but what could he do in their aid?

Rhys had headed back to the trees where he had sheltered for the night. The same misgiving thought was in his mind now. Even if he had use of both his arms, what could he do to find shelter for those two? Yet that was the earl's son, and the girl had wits and courage or she would not have gotten him out of what must have been a slaughterhouse. Though it could well be true, were the child or his body not to be found, there might be searchers out. He sat down on the end of a log. The dull, ever-present pain in his head made it hard to think. And, though he had poulticed his arm that morning, the wound might be slow in healing. As long as it was, he could not draw a bow.

But, there was one thing which they might be able to chance. All that stood against it was his guess that this attack had been the result of long and careful planning. However, if the attackers had sent in spies through the woodlands, all traces of their passing could not have been concealed by men trained to see when even a leaf lay wrong side up on the ground.

Of old the rangers had their own line camps, well concealed and sometimes secret from all save those constructing them. There was a temporary camp not too far from here. Now he might be the only one who knew of it, crude as it was. It would provide shelter, at least.

This Sarita—she was no common keep maid. He had seen her several times trailing that hatchet-faced mistress of hers when they had come to the chief armorer's hall to talk about horse trappings.

And he had heard the countess speak highly of her needlecraft when wearing a new green cloak—the same she had— Rhys shut off that thought quickly.

He came back to the spring in time to see in the far pool a flash of a thin white body. From the splashing and the fact that Valoris no longer lay in the sun, he guessed that the girl had taken them both bathing. The thought of water awoke an itch between his own shoulders, but he had no time for such here and now.

For the moment he sat down to wait. One of the thin stems lay nibbled only on one end and he picked it up to chew, hunching forward to look into the pond. If his hurts had not slowed him down enough to lose his old skill—

With his teeth he pulled back his right sleeve as far as it would go to expose his bare arm. Slowly he inserted hand and wrist into the water, lying belly down and unmoving. There! His hand flipped out of the water and a fish flapped desperately on the land until his fist thudded home on its head.

"How—how did you do that?" The girl's voice was low, as if she feared her question must be a disturbance. He glanced up at her.

" 'Tis an old trick. Most land-born lads know it. But be quiet—"

Valoris had crept forward to investigate the fish and Sarita pulled the child back, offering him some green laves.

"Cress," she said in a half-whisper, and Rhys nodded and turned back to his trout tickling. He lost his second prey, but landed the third.

"A fire?" Sarita questioned. She shivered in the clothes which were clean enough now, but damp and clinging. Rhys nodded. Instinctively he tried to move his wounded arm and then bit back an exclamation. She must have been watching him very closely, for now she came quickly to his side.

"You're hurt; it must be tended." He grimaced. The left sleeve was now sticking tightly over the rude dressing he had put on it. But she was right, he knew enough not to let such a wound go untended for too long. But by the Great Power, he was fortunate that the shaft had merely struck the flesh and not bone.

"Let me see." She was reaching for her belt and now produced a pair of scissors, thin-bladed but, by the look of them, well sharpened. He allowed her to cut away the remnants of his sleeve and

bare the soggy poultice that lay plastered against his flesh. She moved the moss gently aside. At least the skin around the entrance and exit wounds was not red and swollen, though the slightest touch sent a thrill of pain through him.

"What is this?" She was leaning forward to examine the mass of the poultice.

"Something we carry for wounds. But I did not remember it until this morning. It is said to have the property to draw infection from open cuts, and the arrow went straight through."

Sarita turned up her full skirt and cut deftly at the hem, shaking out an even strip.

"There is more in my pouch."

She found it, unlatched the flap, and drew out an open pack at the very top. She raised it to her nose. "Vervaine, and something else—"

"You have herb lore?" That might answer a number of needs.

She shook her head. "Only what I have picked up. We use herbs, barks, and some kinds of roots to dye our own colors. Dame Argalas makes us learn the worth of such early in our training. But I know only a little of the healing herbs and those for the table."

She rested the strip of cloth and the poultice on her own knee.

"Is there any smell?" He must know if there was anything to be feared now.

Obediently she bent her head and sniffed at his arm. "Nothing save the odor of the poultice."

He gave a sigh of relief, a relief which lasted through the torment of her handling and binding, though he tried to control all signs of pain.

"Oh!" As she tied the last knot she looked beyond him and then scrambled, still on her knees, to seize Valoris. In his hands he held one of the fish by the tail and was energetically slapping it against the ground. As the girl jerked it out of his hold, his face puckered, ready for an indignant cry. She spoke hastily:

"Breadie—wait—there is breadie—" He eyed her askance as if he had heard an out-and-out lie. But she held him tightly and tossed the fish to lie beside its fellow.

"Fire—" She was looking at his catch, Rhys thought very wryly, as if she expected him to declare they must choke it down raw—scales, fins, and all.

"We can chance a fire farther in," he told her. "In spite of the rain there is some wood dry enough to use—but it must be a small one."

He felt frustrated as he had to give her orders, doing what he could with his one hand. But at last back at the edge of the burnt land they did have a small fire made among the new grown brush, which would diffuse the thready trails of smoke rising from it.

Under his instructions Sarita set herself to the squeamish business of preparing the fish to be staked on twigs and set at scorching distance from the flames.

The smell of the cooking food was like a sharp awakening for her stomach, and she watched the two dangling fish avidly. But it was necessary also to keep track of Valoris, who was only too charmed by the fire and would perhaps fearlessly reach into it were he free.

6

The fish, shared out and eaten with fingers, was not enough to allay hunger, Sarita discovered. But at least half of hers had gone to Valoris and he was asleep, curled up beside her, his head pillowed on a pile of grass she had pulled. She regarded her hands, dirty, cut by grass edges—surely she would not be permitted by any guildswoman to touch even the meanest of coarse work to be stitched now. Not that there seemed to be any chance at present that she would be offered such refined labors.

"Where now?" Her voice sounded sharp in her own ears, though certainly their plight was none of his making. He was as much a victim of the fate which had struck so swiftly as she was herself.

"There is a ranger shelter not too far away." He was licking his fingers as if to absorb even the smell of the fish they had eaten. "It is rough, but it will be shelter and there are perhaps some emergency supplies there."

"And if they have already found it?" she asked, stubbornly refusing to believe that there could be any end to this dismal roving.

"If they hold the keep, they may send out parties, yes. Especially if they seek the lordling." He glanced at the sleeping child. "But ranger camps have ever been far separated and hidden. Otherwise the wolfheads would have been raiding them for years."

"Wolfheads," Sarita repeated. "Outlaws. But these—aren't they outlaws?"

Rhys shook his head. "No." He repeated to her the stark order he had overheard being given to the ambushers—to leave plundering the dead for the wolfheads.

"Then—who?" There was always gossip to be picked up from the servants at the keep. She had heard scraps during the months she had been working at Var. The earl was a man of power and authority and he had those who envied him, perhaps even held some grudge for a past action. But for any one of the paramount lords to so attack another was an action unheard of these hundred years or more.

"We shall discover who," Rhys replied grimly. "They have us trapped here. If the wolfheads owe them some sort of service, then even the high passages will be patrolled. And the lower one must certainly already be held by them, or they would not have moved on the keep. There might be a way to win through to the west, but not with him." He nodded at the child. "I am liegeman to the earl," he continued. "While I live, his son must be shielded."

For a moment Sarita felt a tinge of resentment. Did he think that she had not already given strength and wit to bring Valoris this far?

"It is a thing," he continued, "that I cannot do without a woman. Since his nurse gave him into your hands, then you stand proxy for her."

Her first thought was to protest that she knew little of child tending, then she realized that this young ranger might know even less. Even though the duty had been forced upon her, she must accept it with the best heart she could.

"When do we move to this refuge?" she asked more quietly. The thought of some reasonable shelter, even if it might be a rude one, was good to consider.

"Let me scout first." The land about them, the ragged half-burnt pasture, might seem utterly deserted, but he would not forget caution, eager as he was to get the girl and child under a roof.

It had been a fair enough day after the night's storm, but that same unease which had gripped him when they had ridden blindly to disaster and death was working in him. He did not feel that they were under any surveillance as yet, the unease was not strong enough to suggest that, but he never wanted again to blunder into such a trap as had caught most of the Var defense force.

In the end he urged her to wake the child and guided them over to another of those stacks of charred logs, closer to the way they must take to their goal. Since until his arm was healed his bow was useless, he left that and his quiver of arrows with her, though Sarita protested she knew nothing of the use of such arms. But when he drew his short-bladed hunter sword and stuck it point-down in the ground before her, she did reach out to curl her hand around its hilt. Sword play she did not know either, but the hide-covered metal in her grasp gave her a small hope of some defense.

She watched him walk out of sight—to her surprise he seemed to be able to melt into the bushes and was gone like a trail of smoke. Each trade had its own arts. Once more she regarded her hands. Luckily Valoris, after a sleepy protest at being moved, had nodded off again.

For the first time, Sarita had a chance to inventory what she had on her person. If there had only been time to bring extra clothing and food. Her skirt was up to her calves now, as she had cut away the cloth to bind Rhys' arm. Her thick-knitted stockings were stiff with mud and ash and snagged, while her soft, indoor shoes showed a gap in the toe of one.

She had her chemise and drawers under her dress. Luckily that was not of a feast day's bright color, rather a rusty brown. Her cap had long since been lost somewhere during her flight. She braided her hair, tying it back with a stout twist of grass.

By her side was the measuring rod. And on her belt—she began to inventory what was slung there. There was her precious needle case in a pouch. She opened it to survey what any embroideress would consider true wealth—some had come from her mother, two a legacy from her grandmother. There were four of true steel (a great treasure) and the rest, varying in size, of bone and ivory, polished by years of use. Her leather thimble sat tucked in with these. She carefully closed the case and put it back in the pouch.

Next hung her scissors in their own case, and beside that a small awl. She hated to think of perhaps blunting those fine blades, but they might need them in the future as tools. Then there was the case which held her spoon and eating knife. And beyond that an affectation meant for gracious living—she grinned wryly at the dangle of small, flower-patterned bags strung on a hoop of bedraggled ribbon, rolling each between her fingers. She sniffed the now-faint odors: spices, dried rose petals, some fragrant herbs, certainly of no use now.

Then there was the small hoop of keys. She had been so proud when Dame Argalas had handed that to her at their departure. Those were useless, too—who cared now about the safety of gold and silver thread, of seed pearls, of precious metal disks? The boxes which had held them all must have been already smashed by looters. But the keys—Sarita shook her head—those might yet be put to some use in another fashion; one could never be too sure about such things. They were metal—she wondered if arrow heads might be made of them.

So, here she was, a needlewoman nearly ready to show some major work of her own hands and achieve the status of journeywoman, thrust out of her position and dashed of her hopes, with a very uncertain future before her. Sarita sighed. To be so removed from everything she knew and understood was in itself a frightening thing if one dwelt upon it.

Rhys used all the tricks of his hard-learned woodcraft as he worked his way to the fringe of the burned area to look downslope over the open fields to the nearest farm. He heard the harsh cries of birds and recognized the naked-headed scavengers of the upper lands. They were clustered, fighting for place, around something downed in the field and the wind uphill brought the stench of death.

He must circle that busy feasting place without disturbing the birds—if he could. Anyone chancing to be on watch would be only too aware of a flock of hookbeaks rising and screaming as they did when anything changed to disturb them eating.

Keeping watch on the birds, he ventured a little northward. He wanted to catch sight of the keep if he possibly could, to see what might be in action there. But he had gone only a short distance before, from behind a stand of trees he had been using for cover, he saw the rise of thick black smoke. The fire must have been lately lit or he would have sighted it sooner.

Under the rush of what was becoming a brisk breeze that column lengthened and veered out to the west. Another stench, even worse—burnt meat! Rhys gagged and fought the bile rising in his throat. He could guess what that meant, but something made him move to make sure.

He wriggled along, belly down, to the top of a small knoll. There was a stretch of meadowland and he could see flutterings here and there which suggested other hookbills feasting, but it was what lay near the keep which centered his attention. There had been erected a great pile of wood. Rhys' far-sighted eyes, part of any true ranger, could see some of that pile was more than forest wood— the legs of what could only be a table slanted into the air in one place.

However, it was what was corded together and heaped on that pile which sent his head down on his arm, his teeth bruising his wrist to keep from crying out in rage. They were burning bodies! He was too far away to recognize more than the fact that there *were* bodies—he could not see any familiar face—but he had no doubt that this was the fate of those who had been in Var-The-Outer when it was overrun.

The same wind which sent the nauseating smoke toward the western hills snapped out a standard on the main tower of the keep. It whipped about, so for a single moment he was able to sight its full color and a part of the device upon it.

Sanghail! But why? What plot had that baron built behind a smiling face and soft voice? He had been a visitor here for hunting in the past season, though he had not liked roughing it enough to really take far to the field himself. It had been his captain of guard who had slain the quadbear Sanghail's lord had claimed for a trophy.

If it was Sanghail, or those under his orders, who were now in Var keep, then the plight of any prisoner was bleak. Rhys began dimly to see a pattern in this. These invaders had already turned the valley into a trap. If they were clever enough, and fortunate, they might even entangle the earl coming home. Then the whole mess could well be blamed on wolfhead dealings, and with the High King not yet crowned, the council might not see fit to move against scattered outlaws for at least another season.

He did not know why he was so certain he had fastened upon what he believed to be the truth of the whole matter, but at that moment he would have taken sword oath he was right.

Which made the burden laid upon him and this sewing girl all the heavier. The young lord's life would be in their hands and there would be an accounting someday, of that he was very sure. There was no use in lying here looking upon horrors now nearly past, it was time to be up and about the duty laid upon him. Rhys slid back through the brush and tall grass and hunched for a moment with his shoulder against a tree, his back resolutely turned on the valley and what lay there.

It was then that he heard the frantic bleating. He identified the sound as a goat—no, two of them and one very young. Plainly they were in trouble. He hesitated. Prudence argued he return to where he had left Sarita and the lordling and get them on the move. But a milk goat—could they continue to feed the little lord on the coarse herbs which might keep them alive but could be harmful for the child?

He headed at last in the direction of the sound and came to a thick patch of briars. A newborn kid, barely able to totter to its feet, butted against the body of its mother, who was struggling vainly to wrest her horns from the hold of some thorned, whiplike branches. She was well entangled and Rhys had to use the sword blade to cut her free. But she stood still while he worked, as if understanding that he was coming to her aid. Plainly she had been a well-tended pet on some farm of the valley.

When he returned to Sarita, he was carrying the kid under his good arm, and an unwieldly burden that was, while the nanny anxiously nudged against his legs from time to time.

Sarita looked wide-eyed at this addition to their party, but quickly took the kid from him. Valoris, waking from his nap, smiled widely and reached out for the small creature. Sarita set it down and it went to feed while the nanny stood patiently looking in their direction as if she was assessing in turn what benefit they might be to her and her child.

However, Rhys was impatient to move on. Sarita tore the strings from the apron still serving Valoris as a kind of blanket cape and tied them around the nanny's neck, giving a gentle tug when she had finished. The goat obediently moved forward as if this was the natural way of things in the world.

Sarita carried Valoris in the sling, giving to Rhys his bow, quiver, and her measuring rod, and so they went. It was a slow pace for the sake of the kid, pausing often—a situation which suited Sarita also, for Valoris was certainly no small weight.

At length they came to the hidden camp, and a well-concealed site it was. Sarita knew that those without wood knowledge might well overlook the small indentation in a thick growth of tall brush and trees which was the doorway. There was a pocket-sized hut, hardly more than a lean-to. Rhys said that he judged it had not been visited since he himself had seen to its closing the season before. There was even a small patch of grass at one side. The nanny needed no urging toward that as Rhys pried open the door latch and waved Sarita inside.

7.

They faced a cramped dark space. Certainly this was rougher shelter even than a farm laborer's hut. Rhys held the door open wide so that Sarita could see about her. There was more than a hint of spiderwebs, and there were mouse-tracks on the floor, as well as a musty smell.

Rhys was at the far wall on his knees beside a large box. When he threw this open, she could see a number of smaller containers which he brought out to line up on the floor. Holding one of these pots between his knees, he screwed open its lid with his good hand and then pushed it toward the girl so she could see that its contents appeared to be clumps of fried fruit.

"Splights," he said. She had a hard time identifying these as the bright yellow and red globes she had seen on market tables.

Already he was working on the second jar, and now she could see it was full of coarse meal. A third held strings of what looked like large twigs but Rhys identified as osdeer jerky.

Sarita eyed this array with inner dismay. She had served her task time with the cook in the guildhouse, but there she had dealt with food fresh from the market, or their own small garden—and one needed pots to cook.

"Pots?" she asked aloud.

Rhys motioned toward the cramped hearth. There was indeed a kettle and pots there, but they would certainly need a good scrubbing, and on a board fastened to the fireplace hung a long shafted fork and a big spoon.

Rhys was back at the storage chest and now had out a roll of cloth. Dust stirred and Sarita pointed to the door. "Out with that—shake it outside." She took the roll from him afterward and discovered she held two coarse blankets. Devising a broom from a branch, she swept out cobwebs. Rhys took a bucket from near the wall and went outside. Sarita hoped that their water source would not be too far away.

She tethered Valoris with a short length of line from the supply box to a stout sapling outside the door, where he seemed content for the moment to watch the goat and her kid.

When Rhys returned with water, she took up the pot and a fry pan she had found and followed, by his direction, a faint path to where there was a stream. There she set about scrubbing the vessels fiercely.

Later she concocted a stew using jerky, some of the meal, and roots Rhys provided after another of his trips away. In addition she coaxed the nanny to yield some milk into a small bowl from which Valoris drank thirstily.

The stew when done smelled better than it looked and she spooned it into the bowl for the child.

After they had eaten, she made Rhys let her dress his wound again, for among their finds had been a packet of the poultices. When she had done he held out his arm, flexing his fingers, moving it back and forth. A shadow lifted from his face. "It heals!"

Once they had eaten and she had coaxed Valoris to sleep on the folded blanket, she had questions she had been too busy to ask before.

"What did you see—in the valley?"

He did not answer at once, nor did his eyes meet hers. Rather he stared at his hand lying on his knee, and she watched the fingers close into a tight fist.

"Tell me!" she demanded.

"Sanghail's banner flies from the keep's tower."

"Sanghail?" That name meant nothing to her.

Now he did look directly at her, and she almost could believe that small points of fire blazed in his eyes.

"His lands border to the south. He has guested many times in the great hall, ridden in the fall hunts."

"A neighbor? One who has shared a bread at a common table?"

Such action broke all custom, both noble and common, beyond belief.

"A neighbor." The knuckles of Rhys' fisted hand now stood out in white knobs. "No wonder the ambush was so well laid."

"And Nurse Halda warned of a traitoress within."

"Perhaps there was more than one such." His voice was cold, grim. "But if any slunk among the guard—or the rangers," now his lip lifted as in a dire wolf's snarl, "they did not profit by it. They burn bodies in the valley—many of them!"

Sarita swallowed, though she thought dully that such news should not have come as any shock. Men had gone to war, towns had been sacked, sometimes all life within them extinguished—but that was of the past. The old High King had enforced peace and held it with the iron hand of impartial justice. When he died, the regents, Earl Florian among them, had followed the pattern he had set.

"The High King is very young." Rhys spoke slowly as if he were trying to work out some puzzle. "The earl and Count Ballas, and the high priestess have held tight reins on all, both nobles and the city merchants—any who have power. There has been loose talk lately that when the young king is crowned, he will allow more freedom.

"Fools!" He slammed his fist down on his knee. "They envy and they believe that with the High Three out of the way they can gain the ear of the king and advance their own desires. What will come is wrangling and war. It has already started—here. Look you—"

He straightened his fingers and leaned forward to draw on the earthen floor while Sarita leaned closer to watch.

"Here is the north pass. It is undoubtedly now held by Sanghail's men. To the south by the river road one can only travel through land where he is birth lord. He has made some kind of a pact with the wolfheads, who know much of the mountains. Yes, Sanghail is now master here—with none to naysay him."

"The earl—" Sarita frowned down at the rude map. Such matters were foreign to her, but she had wits enough to catch the perils which Rhys pointed out.

"It may be long before he learns what has happened. He can

even be involved in some other brawl in the city. I do not believe that Sanghail moves alone. If he had taken the young lordling, perhaps he could have brought the earl to his knees."

"So—?" She realized more strongly than ever how bleak their future was.

"So we are in a prison though we still move freely." He was frowning at the map. "The weather is fair enough—save for the summer storms—and we can find shelter from those. But with the coming of the cold . . ."

Sarita shivered. Winter was sometimes bleak even in the keep. They would not have stayed at Var-The-Outer past the first showing of fall. What would it be like for the two of them and the child? She stared at the cramped cabin and the pitiful accounting of stores before she summed up strength enough for her next question.

"How—how can we fare? We shall need clothing and food and if the cold finds us still here—"

His jaw was set. "Yes." It was a bleak answer and did nothing for her sadly raveled confidence. Then he continued slowly, sharing his thoughts more than trying to reassure her. "I have the forest lore. Once my arm is fully healed for bow work—" Then he was gone from beside her, back to the case of supplies to return with a handful of leather thongs he dangled before her with a flourish.

"Snares," he explained. "Until I am whole, I will show you how to set them. Let me in time bring down an osdeer and we shall have meat for drying and leather. There are plants as well. No, we shall not go hungry. There is only this—none of the other rangers can now be alive. Sanghail wants no witnesses. He is the sort of man who tries to foresee any danger to himself. Thus this woods is unknown territory for him."

"The wolfheads—" Sarita ventured.

Rhys nodded. "Yes, I am not denying that they, too, have knowledge of hunting lore and woodscraft—they will have had to learn it or die. But I think they will withdraw back toward the heights. They will certainly be lacking in wits if they believe that Sanghail will play friend after his use for them is past. This is a very small ranger rest. There are larger, better ones. Some of those may have been found and plundered. It is true, mistress," he said thoughtfully, "that time is now our foe—but it can also be our friend. Look you—they must have searched well for the little lordling and they did not find him. They can be certain no large body of survivors escaped from the keep. If they have some reckoning of all who dwelt there, they will come to know—"

"That I, too, am missing!" Sarita drew a shaky breath. "Janine often hung about the workroom—Dame Argalas ordered her away several times lest she put fingers to our work, she was so curious."

"A girl from the city and a child who has hardly learned his first steps," Rhys returned. "Even if you did win free from the keep, they would not expect you to survive for long. There is no doubt they have overrun all the farms." He thought of the hookbeaks feasting in the meadow and tried not to guess what they might have been tearing at.

They could not have believed in his own survival—*that* had been such fortune as a man might meet once in a lifetime. Nor could they guess that he was now with Sarita and the child, warned of danger and with a knowledge of the land the raiders certainly could not have.

Rhys fingered the snares. They had a chance—no matter how slim it might be, it was still a chance. He studied the girl. She was certainly not skilled in the things of his knowledge, but neither had she wailed or faltered. Yes, they had a chance.

Three days later Sarita learned how precarious was their present safety. The grazing space about the hut was too small for the nanny, so Rhys found a meadow a little beyond where the rangers had once pastured horses, though they brought the goat and kid back to the hut each night.

Sarita went this morning to take the nanny they had named Berry, for the dark spots on her coat, and Briar, her frisky offspring, to this new grazing area. She carried an empty bowl for she had noticed while collecting the animals the previous evening the bright red of ground berries in the grass.

Valoris was content to stay with Rhys, who, making the most use he could of his injured arm, was working at arrow shafts. They were, Sarita thought as she led Berry and tried to avoid the leaping lunges of the playful kid, at least eating well.

Her first attempt at snare setting had brought them two leapers. Stifling her disgust, she had skinned and cleaned the catch under Rhys' direction. And, roasted at the hearth, the meat had given them a lift of spirits.

Once in the meadow, she went down on her knees and began searching through the tangled grass. To her delight there were plenty of the berries ready for harvest.

What it was that first warned her she could not say—it was as if very faint and far away a voice had summoned her. She sat back on her heels, shivering.

Three times before in her life she had heard that summons, and each time it preceded disaster. She wondered fleetingly now why she had not heard it when the keep fell. For the first time—greatly daring—she tried to seek the voice even as it sought her.

It was as if someone held a loomed web before her on which there was a faint design. She could see nothing clearly, though the flesh on her sunburned arms prickled as it might in a winter wind. Then she drew in a breath of pure vileness.

Sarita grabbed out for Berry's tether and jerked the goat back toward the brush ringing the meadow. She kicked against the bowl, sending berries flying, as the goat broke away from her, trotting back to her interrupted meal. Sarita next seized upon the kid. Were she to take him, Berry might follow. But the struggle was a wild one, and when a small hoof painfully grazed her chin, she was forced to free him. She huddled behind the brush screen, trying to make herself as small as possible.

As she watched in dumb terror, she saw the bushes on the other side of the meadow shake. A man stumbled out. He fell rather than seated himself on the ground and sat panting. The rough clothing he wore was certainly not any keep livery, nor was he a farmer, not with the heavy sword sheath, empty though it was, hooked to his belt. His jerkin was furred and ill-fitting, his breeches crudely patched.

He was hatless and a wild straggle of hair fell to his shoulders in greasy strings, while his gaunt cheeks were covered with beard. There was a grimy bandage about his head, but his main wound seemed to be in his side, where another bunching of bandage showed beneath his unhooked jerkin. His hand went to that and he bent over, moaning.

Then he coughed and spewed forth clots of blood, sinking forward, in spite of is struggles, to lie facedown. Sarita breathed shallowly. Though Berry had stopped grazing and was watching him, he had not apparently seen the goat. Nor was he moving now.

Berry snorted and shouldered the kid back in retreat toward Sarita. The girl watched the prone body closely. Then she gave a start and her hand went to Rhys' hunting sword, which he had insisted she carry on any venture away from the hut. The bushes were moving again.

8.

A second man came tramping arrogantly into the open. This was no wounded straggler, drawing upon his last shreds of strength, rather a huge man carrying a bared sword in one hand. Slung fast to his back was a vicious-looking ax. Like the prey he hunted, he was dressed in ragged castoffs, but added to them was the stained surcoat of a keep guardsman and he boasted three unsheathed knives in a sash belt.

"Hookbeak bait!" His hoarse bellow broke the silence.

Then he deliberately kicked the downed man, rolling him over so that he lay face up to the sky. The newcomer dropped to one knee and methodically searched the other, who still lay motionless.

"So you did have it, sneakling!" He held out into the sunlight something taken from beneath the other's jerkin. It gave off flashes of light: a pendant hanging from a chain. Sarita smothered a gasp.

That was a captain's emblem of office. Rhys had said that the plunder from the ambush was to be left for the wolfheads. But the ambush had been days ago. Why—? Or were these ravengers fighting now among themselves over their loot?

The giant gathered the other's belt weapons. With a last kick at the body, he swaggered back into the woods. Sarita felt a strange dizziness—as if that warning of danger had somehow weakened her.

She forced herself to slow and even breathing such as had helped her before. Never had the sendings been so strong before. Nor had she ever mentioned to anyone what she had felt, somehow guessing from the very first time (it had come to her soon after she had been apprenticed, when a live spark from the fire had blazed on folds of cloth) that this was a secret to be kept.

She was sure that the wolfhead was dead. Berry apparently sensed no danger, already at graze again. She must get back to Rhys. If there were wolfheads in the woods so near, then their safety was only an illusion.

Creeping on hands and knees, trying to move without shaking the bushes, Sarita found the unmarked trail. Getting to her feet, she ran for the hut.

Rhys was sitting in the clearing, knife in hand, but for the moment idly watching Valoris placing twigs and shavings in some pattern absorbing to the youngster.

As Sarita burst out of cover, he was on his feet in an instant, snatching up the sword, which had been resting on the ground beside him. He stared at the girl before his attention shifted quickly to the bushes behind her.

Had she needlessly brought down upon them what he could not handle? She looked completely overwrought. He took a stride forward, but he did not move as quickly as Valoris.

"Saree—Saree!" He laughed and ran toward the girl before Rhys could stop him. Catching the folds of her skirt, he stood smiling widely up at her.

"Saree—?" His smile was gone; some of her fear must have reached him.

She stooped and drew him into a fierce hug, as if such contact meant safety for them both.

Rhys drew upon the woodsense bred and trained into him. He felt none of that vague warning of ill which had plagued him just before the ambush. Now he caught at her shoulder with the hand of is wounded arm, in spite of the twinge the gesture cost him.

"What's to do?"

She straightened a little. Her tight grip on Valoris was not now to his lordship's wishes and he was squirming. Rhys saw her visibly swallow, then her answer came as a croak.

"Wolfheads—" she stammered.

He stiffened. Were the three of them to be caught now, they

had very little hope, but what chance he could give to Sarita and the child he would.

In spite of his pain he shook her. "Take the child—go!"

If she had not been seen, perhaps only heard, he would have a very short time to play rear guard.

However, she was resisting his push. "Dead—" He could feel the trembling of her whole body as he shoved her around from the way she had come.

"One—one is dead!" Her voice scaled up even as he spat: "Quiet!"

Valoris was whining and struck out at her.

"Down!" the boy demanded with all the imperious force of his most contrary will.

"One is dead." Sarita had her voice under control now. "The other one—he went back—that way!" She half turned and flung out an arm westward.

"Where is the dead man?" he demanded.

"In the pasture."

"Take him," he waved toward Valoris, "and get out away from the hut. Hide and keep under cover until you hear me whistle." He pursed his lips to produce the call of a flickwing so expertly that he was answered from the bushes. "If I do not return—" he looked at her straightly—"then pray to the Lady, mistress, and do what you can."

Two separate duties tore at him in that moment. His protection was owed to Valoris and incidently to the girl, but he must know what had driven her to such a flight. He felt he dared not make any decision until he saw for himself what lay in that meadow.

Sarita clapped her hand over the child's mouth and headed for the high-growing brush which ringed the clearing about the hut. Rhys tried to shut off thought of what she could do if he did not return—all his attention and skills must be centered on what lay before him.

By the time he reached the pasture, he was somehow sure that the girl was right and there was nothing there to be feared—for the present.

Certainly Berry was browsing contentedly, her kid lying now in the sun-warmed grass, showing no signs of uneasiness. However, on the far side there did lie a body. He edged his way along the green growing wall to reach it.

Had some survivor from the keep taken vengeance?

However, the body seemed to have been roughly searched, which suggested death by the hands of some other member of a pack.

He laid down the sword and rolled the body about under a thick outthrust of briars, hidden as best he could manage. Then he set about tracing the wolfhead's back trail.

To follow that was easy, marked as it was by gouts of blood over which crawled green-bodied flies. There were signs that the fugitive had fallen at least twice. Plainly he had been pursued and now Rhys hunted for signs of that. When he found them, he glanced about quickly, for there were marks of larger and heavier feet both coming and going. The killer had been content to reach his prey and had not gone farther.

The hut was no longer a haven. However, he had never considered it so. They must be moving on.

Now that Sarita had time to catch her breath and think more clearly, she began to hope that the giant had been satisfied with his kill and would not come roving in their direction. She settled herself deep in the bushes, Valoris on her lap.

"Want Hally!" He was growing red in the face and she was afraid that he might burst into a screaming fit.

In desperation Sarita reached up and caught at one of the twigs over their heads. Along it edged a caterpillar, the brown-green of its body so close to the coloring of the twig that it was betrayed only by two bright red spots at the fore-end.

"Look—" Sarita waved the twig before the child. The insect raised its forebody a little, though careful not to loosen its grip on the twig. "Bug," she whispered. "It is going—"

"Home." Valoris' lower lip quivered and began to pucker. She could only guess what the harsh dislocation of his life had meant to him. "Vally go home too!" Again that beginning pucker.

Sarita dropped the caterpillar-laden twig back into the bush to gather him closer. "Someday, little lordling, someday." She won-

dered bleakly if such lies were held against one in that final accounting she had been so often warned of when she was younger.

"Want to go now!" She had only time to clap her hand over
his mouth again to stifle a rising howl.

"Please, little one—"

He was fighting her with all his strength, trying to escape. Sarita
began to rock back and forth.

"There goes the hookyhens . . ." She tried to keep the song to
a whisper.

> "Off to find little Ben.
> They will run and fly and play . . ."

To her great relief the boy stopped his struggling. She had discovered during the past few days that the adventures of the
hookyhens (to which she added with her own imagination) somehow
had the ability to get his full attention.

Valoris' hand unfolded from fists to clap. "Sky!" he crowed.

"Yes, into the sky," she agreed. "They'll ride a cloud by and by."

"Fool!" That word hissed at her startled Sarita so much her
tightened grasp on Valoris brought an instant protest.

Though she could not see him, Sarita knew that Rhys had
returned.

"They are coming?" Her heart began to beat wildly again. She
did not think she would ever forget that hulking giant. Were he to
find them—

"Not yet. But your racket could draw him straight to us. Come,
we must make plans so that we will not be caught."

His sun-browned hand thrust through the wall of greenery and
closed firmly on her shoulder, compelling her forward so that she
scrambled into the open, Valoris with her.

Rhys was not looking at her but rather at the hut. His features
were tight.

"We must move on," he said at last.

"Where?" she demanded. "You say that south and north are
closed to us by Sanghail, and eastward lie the keep lands which he
is surely holding now. To the west are the mountains—the range of
the wolfheads!"

"Not directly west, no. Toward the heights, yes." Having seemingly come to a decision, he nodded as if in answer to a thought of is own. "LodenKail. I think that not even the wolfheads range that peak."

"Monster land," she identified from memories of stories told about the hearth at night.

Amazingly Rhys grinned, and years were wiped from his taut, tanned face. "Monster land," he agreed, as if she had spoken of Raganfors, which she now looked upon as a goal of safety.

"People tell tall tales," he continued, "and have done so for years. What is unknown is always first feared, and if it cannot be understood, that fear grows. I am born of this land, I know of beasts roaming in the heights that no prudent hunter will face. But great monsters—no. Two years ago I went with the boundary markers the earl sent to map the upper lands. We climbed LodenKail—at least halfway. It is but a pile of rocks, to be feared only because of avalanches. We saw a fearsome one which tore away a large spur of forest. I saw the track of a snow cat, a quadbear, but nothing else. Wolfheads are superstitious enough to avoid it—and I think perhaps in the far past there was some lord of Var who told the first tale to make sure there would be some unknown menace to keep rovers out of his territory. I know these woodlands as well as my home hold."

"But perhaps the wolfheads know them well also," she dared to comment.

Rhys was frowning again. "Yes. Well." He spoke slowly as if he uttered every word somewhat against his will. "There *is* something. But I will take sword oath it is not a living, breathing monster." He hesitated for a long moment and then continued. There was a strange expression on his face, as if he were being forced to make a disclosure he dreaded. "We rangers—some of us—" he remembered Gregor and some of the others who certainly had never shown any evidence of such a talent, "can sense when something is wrong—"

Sarita's hand flew to her lips. She could again almost feel that sensation which had startled her in the meadow.

"I spoke once with a scholar sage who was summered here and went boundary marking at the earl's bidding to study and list the living things of this land. He spoke of the fact that certain places exist where events long ago have left a mark which a man cannot see, but rather feels. Also he said that this ability to feel sometimes came in the form of a forewarning."

Rhys' shoulders hunched a little and he darted a quick glance in her direction as if he fully expected to meet with open disbelief.

"A forewarning," she repeated.

Something in her tone brought him to face her squarely. She could feel herself flushing. To betray herself so! His eyes narrowed as he studied her. He asked, "You—you mean you sense things so? At the keep, then—"

Sarita shook her head. "No, not then. But there have been other times, yes. Once there was a fire and I saw—felt—flames before they started up. Then there was the time when a hound kept by the smith in the corner house went mad and ran foaming into the street. But, why did I not feel so in the keep where there the danger was even greater?" She asked that more of herself than him.

He was plucking at his lower lip and seemed to stare beyond her now as if the answer to that might be written on some bush or the wall of the hut itself. And his frown grew deeper.

9.

"**M**ind blinding!" Rhys cried out suddenly. "How else could we have been so easily taken in ambush?" Rhys remembered that the captain had not appointed any outriders that morning—why?

"Mind blinding?" Sarita did not understand.

"Another thing the sage scholar spoke of," he answered with a near impatient note in his voice. "He said it was a demon-born art whereby one with a strong mind could force upon unsuspecting others feelings and sights he wanted them to have."

"Night tales," Sarita scoffed. She could not accept this anymore than Rhys believed in the Loden.

"Halda reported a traitoress," Rhys reminded her. "Was that wench the only hidden weapon? I say that this foul taking of Var keep had been long planned. Sanghail himself is reputed to be learned in old lore, caring more for that than honest sword work."

"But in the meadow I felt evil coming; I was not mind blinded then."

"No, perhaps it was meant to hold only for a short time, or perhaps the effect of it wears off the farther one is from the keep. Yes! Before they sprang that ambush I felt something—not quickly enough to warn!"

A new thought disturbed Sarita, making her hold Valoris closer. "Can one who mind blinds also use such powers to seek?"

"Who knows? But I do not think so, or we would long since have been caught. No, on the slopes of LodenKail one feels uneasy, but—" He shrugged. "I cannot tell you—it must be felt. This much

I do know: we must not remain here. This land may be alive with wolfheads, perhaps searchers also." He was looking at Valoris and she saw him catch his lower lip between his teeth, as she had seen him do before when faced with a problem.

"We shall move by night," he continued a moment later. "There is a hunting lodge in the border hills within a short distance of LodenKail. If the wolfheads or that Sanghail scum have not plundered it, we can equip ourselves much better there."

"How far?"

"Perhaps two nights, maybe more, if we can keep to the trail, but we shall have to travel slowly with him."

Sarita could understand that burdened with Valoris she certainly could not move swiftly. On the other hand, Rhys could not carry the child and act as scout and guard one-armed as he was.

She tried to encourage Valoris to nap while she made up a bundle of foodstuff they could use on the march. When the child was well asleep, she stretched out beside him and also tried to rest. If she knew Rhys as well as she thought she did, he would keep going as long as possible once they had started.

When she awoke later in the afternoon, Rhys drifted noiselessly into sight.

"Nothing?" she asked.

"Nothing."

"Then you must rest." She tried to put authority into her voice. "You cannot guard all day and tramp all night. And you must let me see your wound."

Whether fatigue had caught up with him she did not know, but he obeyed her more meekly than Valoris. To her eyes the wound seemed to be healing well, and he admitted the pain was less and he could move the arm more freely. But he was not easily steered to rest until Sarita evoked what they had spoken of earlier.

If Rhys believed in such a thing as mind blinding, and in his own ability to sense danger ahead, then he must trust that she could also do the same. At last he gave way to her urging.

As the afternoon advanced, Sarita faced west, that mountain with its dark reputation very much in her thoughts. They might be heading into danger. However, Rhys was also right: they could not remain here where at any moment they might be discovered.

Mind blinding. Something in her shuddered away from the thought. How could it be done? She tried to remember those she had known in Var-The-Outer: Halda, her charge, the wench responsible for bringing their meals to the work chamber, the countess, the earl, the housekeeper, various other maids and servingmen.

Janine had seemed, as a nursery maid under the most formidable Halda, a meek and retiring mouse of a girl. She was young, around Sarita's own age, she guessed. And to believe that *she* had this mysterious power Rhys had spoken of was impossible for Sarita. No, there was no one she had known in the keep who could have done such a thing. Yet, looking back now, she could see things which might have made one suspicious that all was not as usual. When the earl had left for Raganfors he had, unaccountably it now seemed, taken with him the most experienced officers of the guards—which had never happened before. And the countess had had that sudden desire to ride out.

Sarita shivered. Was *her* mind giving life to shadows?

She had little time for such profitless musing once they started that night's trek. The girl, with a querulous Valoris in the back sling and leading Berry on a rope, thought by the time she caught a glimpse of dawn she could not take another step.

Rhys led them to crude shelter where there was a standing of tall rocks with an open space in the center. In spite of her weariness, Sarita wondered at that formation, which seemed unlikely to be found in the woods.

"Old Ones' cage," Rhys returned when she commented on it.

"Cage?"

"So we call them. There are a number to be found nearer the mountains. They were certainly raised for some purpose, but those who did so were long gone before our people came here. It may even be some kind of temple."

Sarita stared from one of the upright rocks to another. Were they set so to keep something out—or something in?

To one brought up in the city, the countryside was full of surprises and puzzles. Now, tramping through this wilderness, she felt lonely, even with Valoris whining for attention and Rhys staking Berry on the other side of the largest rock. He had carried the kid

on his shoulders for much of the night. Now released, Briar rushed
to Berry's side.

She was *not* alone. Though she could see and hear those others,
she felt as if she wandered through some maze to which there was
no end.

Sarita was sure Rhys would refuse them a fire, so she sorted out
of the bag of provisions that which could be eaten cold. Rhys had
taken their bowl and was now endeavoring to get a portion of Berry's
milk into it.

It had become such an effort to do anything. After she fed the
child the softest of the food, Sarita leaned back against one of the
rocks and just sat, too tired even to gnaw at the strip of jerky she
held.

Rhys took only a small portion of what she had spread out and
then, laying his sword and bow beside her, said he must take a look
around. Valoris was no longer the stout and sturdy child she had
known days earlier. He was content today to snuggle against her,
one of his hands clutching her torn shirt. She could not keep her
eyes open.

Rhys found a narrow game trail. They needed water—the
leather bottle he had added to his belt was nearly empty—so he
followed it.

The hoof-printed, thready path brought him to a stream. Before
he knelt to rinse and refill the bottle, he surveyed what lay about
closely. Water would draw more than just animals. He had been
very cautious, using a stand of water-wash bush to reach the bank.
On the other side there was a clearing, which was rare in the woods.

He squatted—there was movement over there. Two grazers. Too
small to be of either the two species of deer he knew. Then one of
the brown lumps turned a little sideways and he had a good look
at its head.

He knew that donkey! The lop ear made it memorable to any
who had ever seen it. But at his last sight of it, it had been leading
a pack train taking supplies to the lookout on Hawksknob!

Now he could see a broken hackamore dangling. Lopear's fellow
was belly-banded with a broad strip meant to secure packs. Plainly
the animals were free wanderers. Another massacre somewhere on

the Knob's trail which these two had survived? Or perhaps they had been looted of their loads and turned loose.

The donkeys were forest bred and sure-footed in the heights, and he knew that Lopear answered well to commands. If the looters had had them, why had they not kept animals which could be of service?

He sat very still and tried to open his mind (if it were his mind that controlled that warning talent) to pick up any hints that the two grazing beasts could be bait in a trap.

A newcomer moved out of the woods hedging in three-quarters of the meadow, and Rhys froze until he saw the rise of a curved antlered head. That was an osbuck; and those horns could be vicious weapons. There was no creature more alert to danger than one of these free-wandering males in the season just prior to herd mating.

The osbuck was within an arrow flight, if he could only shoot. But it would be gone the moment he showed himself. He thought of what those donkeys would mean to ease their own journey and knew he had to get them.

Rhys worked his way through the water-wash patch down the bank to where there seemed to be a clutter of water-lapped stone which reached nearly to the opposite bank. Swiftly he shed most of his clothing and lowered himself into the icy flow of water.

With the aid of the stones he won across, though he tripped at the last and sprawled forward, his knees rasping on river gravel as he clawed at the bank. Reaching the top, he lay gasping. His injured arm ached fiercely, and for a moment he feared he had again torn open the wound, but examination proved that fear to be false.

There came a snort loud enough to carry over even the sound of the stream as the osbuck departed in haste. Lopear stopped grazing to stare at Rhys, though his companion continued to eat the newly grown grass.

Would the donkeys take to their heels as had the osbuck?

Rhys stood where he was. Lopear advanced several steps, his head up, ear flipping as he suddenly shook his head and uttered a loud bray. That aroused his companion, who also turned to regard the man.

Then, to Rhys' joy, Lopear trotted confidently toward him as if answering some summons he was well used to obeying, and his companion fell in behind him.

Lopear arrived directly before Rhys, uttering a second bray. The ranger ventured to catch at the dangle of hackamore. Remembering what he had seen the train captain do days ago, Rhys lifted his aching arm so he could scratch Lopear at the tuft of upstanding mane between his ears.

The donkey bumped his head against the man and once more brayed, his companion standing a little away as if he were not quite sure about such meetings.

Rhys, keeping a tight hold on the short rope, gave the starting call of the packers: "Ooooheee—push!"

Lopear followed easily and his companion fell in behind. Rhys half expected him to balk at the stream. He gave a strong pull to the rope and slipped back down the bank. Lopear followed in an ungainly fashion, striking the water with a great splash. They made their way along the line of stones which slowed the force of the water until they managed to pull out again. Once on land Lopear swung around, jerking the rope out of the ranger's hand to look back at the water with what seemed to Rhys to be a look of complete disgust. Rhys found himself laughing as he had not done since that morning of death and disasters.

Lopear and his companion—whom Rhys named Mouse, as his color was that of that creature and he was slighter and smaller than Lopear—made no effort to move away as Rhys wiped himself with handfuls of grass and then redressed.

They squeezed back along the game trail, the ranger more hopeful now of the future than he had dared to be before. Here was the answer to their creeping pace. Valoris could ride one of the donkeys and they could put their supply pack, and any game he was able to find, on the other. Perhaps fortune was turning a fair face upon them.

Thus at nightfall they did journey at far more than the crawl of the previous night. That the donkeys were docile and biddable was great good luck.

Sarita walked beside Valoris, who was mounted on Lopear, with one hand out to steady him. Though they stopped several times during the night, she herself felt far more able to keep going. However, they were very close to the end of the supplies they had brought and Rhys knew that he must turn to hunting. They could set some snares when they camped, but day-set traps were never as productive as those set at nightfall. He constantly exercised his arm. Oddly enough, in spite of the strain he had put upon it at the river, he was better able to use it now.

Three such nights of travel brought them to landmarks Rhys knew well. Again he scouted ahead, as the lodge was closer to the mountains. He was more than half convinced he would find it had been looted, or was in the possession of the enemy. Yet all was peaceful and quiet, as it had been the last time he was there.

He scouted very carefully before he brought them to the large cabin. Berry, Briar, and the donkeys were turned into a small, fenced pasture. Rhys unfastened the intricately knotted latchstring of the door. They came into a dark room with shuttered windows. He made no move to open them.

"Stay!" he ordered Sarita as she stood behind him with Valoris in her arms. She could hear him moving and then saw a spark of light flare up, flame being held to a candle inside a lantern.

After their all-night trek the light seemed bright enough as Rhys bore the lantern about. There was more than one room, he showed Sarita: two behind the large one, one containing a single large bed and the other with bunks against the wall.

A large stone basin was mounted beneath the end of a pipe in the wall. Rhys held the lantern closer and used his knife to wedge out some plug there. A slow trickle of water splashed into the basin and found its way through another pipe in the floor. Sarita expressed amazement at such a nicety.

Now Rhys opened cupboards. Inside were rows of sealed jars. No meager storehouse here. He at last put the lantern down on the table and brought out an armload of wood from a hearthside box, laying a fire.

"Dare we?" Sarita broke the silence which had held her since she had entered.

"For now—yes," he answered without turning his head.

She placed the weary child on a settle by the fire and went to investigate the contents of some of those jars, her mouth watering at the thought of food enough to satisfy them all.

10.

One day slid into another, so that it was difficult for Sarita to keep track of time. The keep seemed very far behind as she worked to make the most of the supplies in the lodge, hoping to be better prepared if they must take to the road again.

She discarded her tattered clothing for ranger dress, feeling a bit shy when she first drew on breeches and a jerkin, but rapidly becoming used to and enjoying the freedom they gave her. For Valoris, since the weather was now summer indeed, she fashioned tunics which left his arms and legs bare to the sun. She also produced a small harness which could be attached to a leash of sorts so that he might enjoy the outside with the animals while she was busy, and yet not stray too far.

Rhys insisted that she learn the use of one of the spare bows, but she showed very little skill. Oddly enough she did much better with a sling, being able to bring down a leaper, or even meadow fowl on the wing, four times out of five. Sarita also gathered any plant which had use, as well as berries as they ripened, but she never went too far from the lodge.

Sometimes when she had a very brief idle moment she would study her hands. Her fingers were so rough now Dame Argalas would never let her touch any fabric of value. Would she ever return to the old life? Her doubt concerning that grew stronger each day.

Rhys went off on scouting and hunting trips, but he discovered no sign that there was any interest in the lodge. Still he always insisted that she go armed. Her days were spent at such labor that she slept heavily at night, wearied by all she had done and what would face her in the morning.

Valoris was flourishing. His dimpled baby roundness was gone and he was growing fast. The light curls, which Sarita had cut so that they would not get entangled in a bush during his exploring, faded to a very pale yellow. Watching him as he played beside Briar and walked with Lopear, Sarita wondered if a living Halda would have recognized her charge.

He no longer screamed with temper when his will was crossed, eagerly following Rhys whenever the ranger was there. But at dusk he was quick to find Sarita so that she could hold him and sing some of the nonsense songs she dredged out of her memory, or tell made-up stories about Berry and Briar, and even the grass-dwelling insects which always interested him.

It grew too hot by midday to stay outside. Sarita had to retreat within the shade of the cabin to work on the canvas bags she was stitching together for the donkeys. Sometimes she brought in some meadow flowers—their color was a pleasure to the eye, and she longed for a pen and a scrap of parchment to set down their delicate shapes. Once Rhys found her busied with a piece of stripped bark and a charred stick. Having watched her efforts for a minute or so, he went to one of the cupboards to return with a packet of thin strips, which he spread out on the table. There were no brightly colored pictures on these—just lines and dots.

"What—?"

"Maps. See?" He leaned across the table. "We are here." He stabbed down a finger. "These were left by the sage scholar when he returned to the city. "I know, mistress, you can put down the likeness of a flower. I know you wrought needle magic for the countess' green cloak. Now—there are marks on this," he touched the edge of the first sheet, "which the sage did not explain. Nor did our captain understand why these were left with us. If there is any meaningful pattern here, perhaps you can read it. For if time brings danger, this is the direction in which we must go."

The shutters were open and a band of sunlight crossed the strip. Sarita squinted down at the markings.

At first glance there were only scattered dots and two kinds of wavering lines. She traced both and found nothing in them she could understand. Then she lifted her head to view the strip from another angle.

"What is this?" She pointed to a circle of much finer dots, hardly more than pinpricks.

"The stone cage," he identified.

But already a pattern was beginning to appear. She pulled her awl from her belt and used it to leave a faint indentation on the parchment. "See—you have a triangle!"

"Or an arrow! And it points straight to LodenKail. Therefore there is more importance in the circle than we knew."

"Or at least your scribe scholar thought so," she answered.

She had been holding the awl point down over the strip. Now she gave a small cry. It was as if some giant, invisible fist had closed about her hand and was forcing it beyond her own will, while in her that suggestion of distant danger stirred.

The awl point did not follow the triangle of the stones, rather it was being jerked, until she could no longer fight it, toward the other side of the map. She heard a deep breath, almost a gasp, from Rhys.

"East—east to the keep!"

"Not—not by my will," Sarita protested. "Stop it! Rhys—hold me—"

He eyed her narrowly. "Mistress . . ." He raised his own hand from the tabletop and his fingers swept through the air, but not toward her.

Sarita was shaking. The awl no longer moved, but was rather poised above one point on the map. She could not withdraw it. "It is—it is bewitched!"

"No." Rhys spoke slowly, with a note of awe in his voice. "Mistress, of what breeding are you?"

Sarita was still struggling against the immovable awl. She answered impatiently: "What matters my line, ranger? Family blood has nothing to do with this!" She was very close to tears, her fear so very strong.

Suddenly the awl dropped, stuck deep through the parchment and into the table. She was free and grabbed back her hand, nursing it against her breast as if it carried some dripping wound.

"But it does." He had both fists planted on the table and was leaning over her. "They say that the old gifts have long gone, yet perhaps that is wrong. Time does not erase everything. My mother had the Sight—to a much greater degree than I have. She could talk to plants and they grew the better. And she was a healer. What of your kin, mistress?"

Sarita tensed; some of what he said she did not understand at all. "The guildswomen—they do not marry by life oath. If they do, they lose their standing. My mother was a noted embroideress. She did the great banner of the High King and she died of the winter fever the year after I was apprenticed. I never saw much of her, for I was fostered by the house. I know very little save she was honored for her work. She grew only the plants needed for dyes and certainly she never talked to them—nor was she a healer. I do not know what you mean."

"Were there no tales in the city of the Old Learning?" He appeared utterly surprised.

"We had no time for tale-telling—though there were stories of the great houses and their jealousies and of the court, yes. But of Old Learning I have never heard."

"Perhaps then it is only in the country that such lingered. We both know that we can foretell danger. And I have heard of other things—"

"Such as mind blinding?"

"Your awl, mistress, the handle gleams. Of what is it made?"

"Silver," she returned a little proudly. "It was my mother's, given her in honor of her work when she was not much older than I am now."

"Silver," he repeated. "Do you not know that silver is the metal esteemed by the Old Learning, that it is said at times to obey laws we do not understand? And who was your father?"

Sarita shrugged. "It does not matter to a guildwoman. I heard once from a maid that he was a far traveler, a man from overseas who dealt in pearls and came to the guildhouse to sell. It does not matter. I am Sarita Magasdaughter, of that I can be proud."

"However, what you have just done, Sarita Magasdaughter, is a power search. Where your silver-headed tool touched—there is a source of power. And it touched on the keep. Thus we can now be sure that Sanghail has other weapons beside steel and arrows."

Sarita hastily plucked the awl free. She was almost inclined to throw it from her. She did not want ever again to be so used by something she could not understand. But no, it was her mother's and it would continue to hang at her belt. But to use it—she would be of two minds over that.

Rhys was studying the map. "An arrow point—stone circles set up in the old days—"

"Perhaps." She got up. "It is a warning. In that way danger lies."

She hoped he would accept that and think no more of LodenKail.

"We shall see. I am for another look around." It was as if her experience with the awl had made him wary again. "Keep close— bring Valoris in."

"But food—it is time—"

To her surprise he shook his head. "I shall eat when I return. Hold to your mind warning, mistress. We may have need of all such talents before long."

Talents he called them, she thought resentfully. Her talent was with thread and needle and she wanted none other to plague her. A shiver ran through her. She raised her hand and worked the fingers which had held the awl in that painfully tight grip. She wanted none of that again.

Having made a circle about the lodge, Rhys headed resolutely eastward. That sewing girl might not believe in talents, but he did— at least enough to want to look at the valley and see what was going on there. The performance of her awl suggested a new deadliness which they might have to face.

He was well along when he crossed a wide, open trail. Those who made the trail were assuredly not woodsmen, and it was very plain to read. There was one ridden horse in the party and he was able to puzzle out footprints of some half-dozen men.

They were not heading west but rather in a northerly direction, and he followed, wishing to make sure they did not double back. The trail was more than a day old, and at length he came to a small glade where they had camped for the night.

Wolfheads, unless they were rich with plunder, would not go shod in hide boots. The prints he followed were uniform, therefore he deduced they were a party of soldiers, though ones that were not well disciplined. Flies buzzed above a pile of offal from some small kills, as well as above even more noisome leavings.

Still, he decided to keep on for a space, eager to know who and what these invaders were.

He almost stumbled over a body shoved half under a bush. The sight of the green-dyed jerkin and the darker green of the breeches made his breath catch for a moment. Then he forced himself down on one knee to roll the limp form over. The face had been battered nearly to a pulp, and there were stains elsewhere. He had died hard.

Tufts of blood-soaked hair led Rhys to an identification. Shamus had been noted for his hair—as white as that of a grandsire when he was not yet into his twenties. He had been stationed at the Lookout—what was he doing here?

There were rope burns on his wrists, though those were now free. His jerkin had been torn from its hooks to show blood marks across his shirt; some of those stains were older than the others.

Had Shamus been trying to reach the keep and been gathered in by a Sanghail scouting party? Or had he been taken prisoner at the Lookout and, for some reason, brought along? His badly battered head suggested that his captors must have lost patience with him for some reason.

Something reflected the sun's light from inside one of the dead man's hands, now balled into fists. Rhys worked patiently to open the stiffened fingers. At last he held up a broken chain. Attached to one of its links was a night-black stone. The thing had either been carved by some inept hand or perhaps rudely shaped by time and nature itself.

As he held it closer, Rhys stiffened. It was in the form of a monster's head, and the longer he stared at it the sharper its features grew. When his hand inadvertently touched it, he felt as if he had fingered loathsome slime. With an oath he threw it from him.

It had the guise of an amulet. Many men wore such fortune charms—but this was not meant to attract any good luck. And he was sure that this was no possession of Shamus. Perhaps in his death struggle he had torn it from one of his captors. Rhys took a sudden chance and loosed his warning talent. Nothing answered him, save that he knew this thing was a danger worse than a bared sword or an expert archer's shaft.

He drew his knife to cut a small branch from the bush and used the tip of it to hook the chain. With that lump of nastiness a-swing, he went back to the abandoned camp, plunging the stone into the ashes of their fire, dropping bits of charred wood on top.

As for Shamus—he had no way of burying the ranger. To do so would awaken suspicion if those murderers returned this way. But he went to stand over the body and fitted an arrow into the torn shirt across the now stilled heart.

> "Wide and smooth the trail.
> Fair the day, still the night.
> Duty's son, this be thine
> Pass swiftly beyond all time."

His voice was strained, but he was sure he had correctly remembered the proper words of farewell, though he had heard them only once before.

There was a rage rising in him. He wanted to follow this trail, perhaps lay an ambush of his own to bring down those who had slain his comrade. Shamus had not been a close friend, but he was a ranger and by the old truth his blood debt now rested on Rhys.

But he dared not be so reckless. There was the young lordling and the girl. Let him be taken as Shamus was and sooner or later their portion would also be death. Duty turned him back though he deliberately struck farther east as he went.

11.

Rhys neared the thinning edge of the woodland. The fields below were hedged and might provide some cover. He could see the roof of a farmhouse—only there was an odd slant to the roof. He realized a portion of it was missing. The building must have caught fire, while the fields showed no cut of a plow, grass growing over old furrows.

Sanghail must have laid waste widely, not attempting to preserve the keep holdings. Rhys accepted that roof as a warning and slipped back into cover.

It was very late afternoon as he fell into a trot. Still, he did not head toward the lodge but wove a pattern back and forth to throw off anyone who might chance upon his trail. Taking every short cut he knew, he moved at a steadily increasing pace.

As the hours passed, Sarita had lost none of her uneasiness. When the afternoon shadows lengthened she made sure Valoris was in the lodge, but she had no way of sheltering the donkeys and goats from observation. She could only trust that the animals might be considered strays by any lurker.

During their first day here Rhys had shown her the one hiding place. It had not been intended as such, though there was always the threat of an attack by wolfheads, especially in winter when the starving time came. Rather it was an extra storage arena under the floor of the larger bedroom, to be found only by counting boards and inserting a knife point to raise the catch of a trapdoor.

Sarita closed and barred the lodge door, then struggled the inner shutters into place. Her hands were bruised and she lost a portion of a fingernail before that was done.

Valoris watched her, remaining quietly where she had put him down. It seemed almost as if her rising apprehension engulfed him also. She lit only one of the lanterns before she ladled out the stew which had been bubbling away for nearly an hour.

What if Rhys had been captured—or was dead? That he was gone so long was a bad portent. She fed the child, though she could not put her spoon into her bowl and finally emptied its contents back into the pot.

"Lady," she said, "oh, Lady! Be shield and sword for us this night!" She knew that she was voicing the plea not only for the child and herself but for Rhys.

Gathering Valoris into her arms she began to sing, softly to make sure her voice would not carry beyond the log and stone walls about her.

> "Little lamb, day is done.
> It is home we have come.
> Safe we rest within Her arms,
> Little lamb, close thy eyes,
> Dream well of a fair morrow's skies."

Valoris nodded until his head rested against her shoulder, but she did not carry him to the large bed they shared.

She no longer mouthed words half remembered from Halda's crooning. No, somehow tonight she had no desire to seek a bed for herself. There was—

Just as it had struck at her in the meadow by the hut so did the dark warning come!

Around her the lodge room blurred. She blinked, and blinked again. What she saw was the great hall of the keep as plain as if she stood there, not far from the dais! There were two before her on that dais. One was small of stature, richly dressed and yet with something meager about him. However, the other beside him, standing with one hand on the high back of the seated lord's chair, bending forward as if he had been in low conversation, but now glancing up full at her.

"Lady!" She had not screamed that aloud, though her throat ached as if she had.

The sparse, bone-narrow figure raised a hand from which a large sleeve fell back—a near fleshless hand. The head was cowled and she could not see any feature—except—except eyes—eyes which held her captive.

It—it wanted her—no—the child!

Sarita knew that as well as if it had shouted an order. The child—she was to bring the child.

Then the vision wavered, and she was once again in the lodge. But holding her was that compulsion which the eyes had set upon her. Sarita wavered, feverishly seeking some help. She was on her feet, Valoris in a tight hold. He awoke with a cry of pure fear, twisting so that she had to fight to hold him.

"No!" Sarita swayed forward, but she did not take the step the force urged upon her, nor the next which would bring her to the door. "No!" she screamed to what she could no longer see, but which held her in bondage.

"Lady!" She tried to hold in mind that banner in the chapel— that wonderful tapestry of the Fair Power in all Her glory. "Lady!"

For one dazzling moment she did see—the tapestry—moving as if She who was pictured there was stepping down into Sarita's world.

"Lady!" She staggered back. The release from the pressure nearly took her from her feet. She laid the child down, kneeling over him, fumbling with the tools at her belt, drawing out the awl. Its silver knob blazed with more than the reflection of the dying fire. A cold radiance surrounded both of them.

This time no force compelled her, rather it was dawning knowledge, sudden and sure, as if a needle moved with perfect stitching along a guideline.

Still she sensed that other trying to reach her, to bind her will. Then, as suddenly as a sword could snap a thread, it was gone and a moment later the radiance flickered out.

Sarita continued to huddle where she was. This had been such a battle as she would not believe could have existed had she not fought it. What evil aid had Sanghail summoned to the taking and holding of Var-The-Outer?

Valoris was looking up at her wide-eyed. Tears welled in his eyes. Sarita gathered him close again. That—that *thing* had tried to make her its tool in order to secure the child!

"Lady!" Something she had never tried to reach before was filling her—belief in powers unseen which could help, be summoned!

Slowly she returned the awl to its belt loop. However, her thoughts had moved beyond the two of them here. If that *thing* had found their refuge, what of Rhys? She knew very little of men save what she had observed when they came and went at the guildhouse, and the few she had known at Var-The-Outer. She did not know how one measured the worth of a man. All she knew was that Rhys was now a part of her life, and if he were lost, she would feel the loss more than any she had known before.

Where was he—was he still alive? She shrank from that thought. He must be alive, for she had a queer feeling now that if Rhys were dead she would somehow sense it, even if she never saw his body.

Now a calm began to enfold her like a warm cloak. Certain that the peril was gone for now, Sarita took up the child and, taking off his earth-dusted clothing, put him to bed.

He had relaxed and his eyes had closed peacefully when she drew the covers over him. Sarita returned to the outer room and swung the pot of stew back toward the fire. Sooner or later another would come to eat it, someone hungry for a long trail.

She could not settle back to her work of making another shirt for Valoris. Rather she stirred the stew now and then and listened—always listened.

What she waited for came at last: that low whistle he had taught her to listen for. Sarita moved quickly to draw the door bar.

Rhys did not open the door very far, but rather squeezed around its edge and shut it quickly, at once dropping the bar into its hooks. He had not uttered any greeting and Sarita watched him narrowly. The lantern light did not reveal his features too clearly, but she knew that something had happened to change him. Had he too been summoned?

The ranger drew a deep breath and the tension in him eased a little. Then he was staring at her and his demand came quickly.

"What has happened here?" His gaze shifted over her shoulder as if he expected someone to move out of the shadows to join them.

She had not meant to blurt it all out, but now the words escaped her and she told him of the vision of the keep and the compulsion laid upon her by that summoning hand.

"It wants Valoris! Rhys, what evil of the dark is against us now?"

"I can guess no more than you." He shook his head slowly. "This day I found death—and the tracks of those who dealt it. How much they may have learned from him—that I cannot guess either. But that you were discovered here!"

"Who was that I saw with Sanghail? Do you think it will try again to trap me—or send others?"

"Somehow they have learned where we are. We must move on."

"Tonight?" She was not sure they could do it. Rhys looked very tired—he must have food and some rest. And she must pack as much as she could to make the journey more endurable.

To her relief he shook his head as he turned to set his bow in the rack. Then he went to splash in the basin of water and make use of the coarse towel hung nearby before he settled at the table and spooned up the stew Sarita had waiting for him. She filled the bowl a second time before he shook his head.

"This one you saw with Sanghail. You have never seen his like at the keep?"

She shivered. "No, nor do I want to again."

"I know of the Lady." He was eyeing her intently. "Hers is not a creed we of the forest follow, though we agree that some purpose rules the life of men, animals, all growing things. What we take of life we must in time return. Perhaps that force is your Lady. I am willing to give thanks to *Her* this night. What walks this land now is more than just clean death. Here—give me one of your drawing sticks and a piece of bark. I have not your skill, but at least I can try."

Sarita supplied what he asked for. He used the charred twig with care, stopping many times to inspect the drawing, once or twice muttering a word of impatience or frustration. At last he pushed the bark in her direction.

"You are from the city, and cities often breed dabblers in things beyond the proper laws. Tell me, mistress, have you ever seen the like of this?"

It was certain he was no artist, but the longer she studied it the more she began to see what he had been trying to reproduce. It was— She felt a sickness rising in her. This was not only monstrous, but somehow it seemed as if a thread of evil spiraled up from it. The outline was a head, but of no human kind, yet somehow fouly akin.

"I have not—" she began, when memory stirred. There was a dim corner of the Great Fane in Raganfors into which she had once wandered while waiting for the Arch Deaconess to write an answer to a message from Dame Argalas. On the wall, half hidden by a standing screen, there had been a queer carving. She had found it while she was tracing the pattern on the screen and for the first time in her life had been frightened by something which had no life.

"There is a carving, like this, in the Great Fane. It was in the Chapel of Ungwine the Shaker—meant I think to represent one of the demons she drove back to the Deep Dark."

"Then there are those hereabouts who have hauled that demon out again." He told her of Shamus and the finding of the amulet. "They were heading north toward the pass, away from us. So far Fortune of the Lady favors us. But with the morning we must go— keep on the move lest we be caught in some trap. Get your rest, mistress, you shall be needing your full strength!"

Sarita went to the inner room. The sound of the child's even breathing was disturbing for a moment. It reminded her too strongly of what leaving the lodge might mean. Now she was sure Rhys would hold to his plan of going westward to LodenKail. Though why he would head toward such a territory when they were already threatened she could not understand. On the other hand, Rhys and his woods knowledge were the only hope for her and Valoris' survival.

Suddenly she caught up the awl from her belt and on impulse drove the point of it into the head of the bed so that it stood fast over where their two heads would be pillowed.

She feared sleep—could that beckoning thing reach her when she was so lost to defenses? However, she dared not go without rest when a long journey lay before them. Sighing, she crawled into bed and gathered Valoris against her. Sleep came swiftly.

They had left the shutters up and she had no way of telling how late it might be when a knock at the door awakened her. Valoris rolled across the bed, and she caught him just in time to make sure he had sandals and shirt on before she dressed herself. As she came into the great room, she smelled the heartening scent of frying meat. Rhys was wielding a long-handled fork to turn strips in the frying pan. On the table was a bowl of berries and a cup of goat's milk. Sarita just had time to keep Valoris from grabbing that before he spilled it.

On one side of the floor there were two long strips of water-proofed cloth laid ready. Covering for packs, she understood. It would seem that Rhys had already been very busy, for there were other supplies laid out along with small bundles of clothing.

"We travel by day, then?"

The ranger brought the meat to the table.

12.

"What of the wolfheads?" It would be long before Sarita forgot—if ever—what she had seen in the meadow.

"Men can be fought," he replied grimly. "There are few among those sulkers who have ranger knowledge of this land. They also may no longer look to Sanghail for leadership. He has used them for his purpose—they have looted the valley. He has his own men to provide for. If they grow bold, then he may turn to hunting *them*—and show no mercy.

"In the past the earl put himself to the trouble of aiding at least three outlaws I know of—men who were forced into the wild by ill fortune. I wonder if those can now be counted among his enemies?"

They turned to packing. Valoris, excited by the chance of again riding Lopcar, asked constant questions which Sarita, busy helping Rhys secure packs, answered as best she could.

They had what extra clothing she could bundle small enough, pouches of jerky and dried fruit, and some of the meal. But it was impossible to take all she knew they should have.

Rhys worked three bows into the ties of the packs, with two quivers full of arrows to join them.

The day's midpoint had been reached before their preparations were finished. Two leather bottles of water were slung over Lopear just in front of Valoris' perch, and Berry submitted to a neck rope, but there was a wild rush to secure the kid. Rhys knotted closed the latch of the lodge door.

For a time the going was easy, for they used a trail hunters had taken for several seasons. It was Sarita's task to see to the small caravan while Rhys scouted ahead.

She had learned something of tracking and the earth here was marked only by the slot of buck and, once, a broad pad fringed at one end with indentations of claws. Rhys identified that as the print of a curven cat—a creature which would flee men rather than attack.

The dusk that always hangs beneath the trees deepened. They must find a camping place soon. That thought had no more crossed her mind than Rhys appeared to wave them on. She could hear the murmur of water and they came out on the edge of a stream of some width. Did Rhys expect them to cross that?

No, for as he stood waiting them, he motioned westward. Through the green she could see the gray shapes of moss-mottled rocks—another of those cages? But certainly they had not come as far as the second she had seen marked on the map.

These did not form a circle, rather a triangle, and within was a pavement of sorts—stones roughly fitted together. At the far point was a firepit in the crude flooring. There was room within for them and the animals both, but after they had unloaded the donkeys, Rhys let them and the goats out to graze.

"What is this place?" Sarita busied herself with their food supplies.

Rhys shook his head. "Who knows? It is another of the Old Places. The sage scholar was much interested in them. He wanted to get men and supplies and come again to study these. This was never roofed, I believe—whoever raised this preferred an open sky overhead."

"Well enough in summer and when there is no rain," the girl commented. "But with that or snow—" She gave an exaggerated shiver.

Yet in her the feeling grew that they were intruding, that this was not a place where they or their kind were welcome. Still the stones were apparently so ancient that she thought no one would now rise to refuse them shelter.

Rhys carefully built a fire and cooked them a warm meal. Valoris nodded off to sleep, a fistful of dried fruit still in his hand. Sarita settled him in the blanket nest she had made.

Rhys crouched by the fire only a step or two away. The night

was so still she could hear the movements of the animals outside
and once the deep-throated cry of a winged night hunter. She settled
down beside the ranger.

"We do not belong here."

He turned a little to meet her eye to eye.

"You feel that also? No place for us—still, there is no warning."

He paused and she tried to shift her own thoughts to discover
a name for the feeling which gripped her.

"No warning," she agreed, "just old—old, and not of our kind.
Did your sage ever return to search? Was it treasure he would hunt?"
She turned her head. Behind her, in this faint light, the stones
looked unpleasantly like broken fangs.

"No. He was old and I think that once back in Raganfors he
felt such journeying too much for him. As for treasure, he mentioned perhaps finding some things which could give clues to the
builders. If he had mentioned treasure, there would have been half
a hundred men out in a day with axes and spades." Rhys, as he so
seldom did, laughed softly. "Treasure is always a potent word to set
men to laboring, mistress."

Her next words were far from the subject. "Why do you call
me mistress, ranger? We are no longer in the keep."

"Or bound by its customs?" he asked. "I do not know, save that
I know little of women and I thought you might believe me overbold
to use your name without asking."

"I am Sarita Magasdaughter, as I told you, and you are Rhys,
one who knows his trade well. We of the guilds honor a good jour-
neyman. Shall we have less custom between us now?" She did not
know why she wanted to hear him say "Sarita" rather than the more
proper "mistress."

"Well said, Sarita. Now, I am for first watch. Sleep well, there
is a long trail tomorrow."

He moved from the fire and she rolled up beside Valoris, somehow pleased to have heard him say her name.

On the fourth day after they left that ancient rock formation,
the weather turned against them and it began to rain. The trees
under which they now moved kept off some of the water, and this
was no great storm such as had struck earlier. But it was enough to
make one miserable. Sarita slogged beside Lopear, tugging at Berry's

rope, for the nanny was expressing her dislike of the weather by trying to halt now and again.

They were drawing close to the mountains, which to Sarita promised more trouble than refuge. The two past night camps had been without fires in improvised shelters.

So far Rhys had discovered no traces that any of their kind had come this way. Yet Sarita remembered that this was wolfhead land, and she noted that Rhys moved with extra caution.

They were traversing the foothills. Beyond loomed the frowning bulk of LodenKail. She kept her head down under the drive of the morning rain but she knew it was there—waiting.

Valoris whined. She had wrapped him as best she could against the rain and, as she walked beside him, pointed out things which might catch his attention, though there had lately been no noisy outbursts of temper from the child. She remembered how he could keep a corridor ringing with his enraged clamor, and they certainly must have no such screams from him now.

"Go home—want Hally—want sweeties—bad Saree—go home!" It was a miserable little litany and she only wished she could indeed give him all he asked for. Looking back she was surprised that the child had held up as well as he had during the hardships into which he had been plunged.

"Good boy. Soon—soon we shall be there—"

At least there had been no more of those attacks to stifle her will and make her obedient to the purpose of the Dark. Rhys must be right—it had centered on her at the lodge because of the strange behavior of the awl. She still found it difficult to believe that she had had anything to do with such happenings.

Rhys came into view again. He did not disappear as he usually did, but waited for them to join him.

"North."

"Why?" Sarita asked after she had taken a good view of the country. That way was broken by ridges and many rocky outcrops. There was certainly no trail and to work their way through would be a hard journey.

"Fresh trail to south and east," he reported tersely. "If we can mend our pace, we can be well away by nightfall. There is a way up the mountain—I have found its opening."

He stayed with them, urging Lopear to a trot as he steadied Valoris. Berry balked and Sarita had to coax her on by giving her half of one of their precious meal cakes.

She began to feel oddly dizzy—trees and stones wavered as she moved up this rise and down that. At least she was wearing ranger boots instead of her worn-out slippers and, though the rain water squished in them, she did not feel every stick and pebble she trod on.

At last she realized that they were following a trail of sorts. Every once in a while Rhys brought their procession to a halt while he stepped away to study the trunk of a tree. The third time he did this, Sarita pushed up beside him. What kind of guide was given by trees?

His fingers were pressing the bark at eye level and she saw there a faint scarring, nearly grown over and certainly to be noticed only by one diligently searching for it.

"We marked out way to LodenKail two years past," he told her.

Her fear of what lay ahead was growing steadily, perhaps made worse by that strange struggle at the lodge. Deliberately now, knowing she *must* know the worst, Sarita forced open the mind door she had tightly closed and sent out a small, seeking tendril.

Instantly she recoiled. She swung upon the ranger. "There is something—it waits—"

He stood very still and closed his eyes, his face turned in the direction she had pointed.

"Yes—but not what you fear, Sarita. This is the edge of Loden-Kail. I felt this before when we came here. It does not mean harm—"

No harm? she thought angrily. *He* had not faced that *thing*! Perhaps it was now lying in wait, readying for them. Still, what she had touched had not had an overpowering sense of evil. However, did not humans smile or frown at will? What threatened before could now entice.

Her hand went to the awl. She stepped away from him and once more reached out with her mind.

No, this was not evil—or at least not any evil her human blood shrank from. Rather, it was akin to what she had felt in the circle of stones. *Old—old—*that one word beat upon her. "It is like the stones—very old."

"Yes," he agreed. "True, it might be a set warning, but either not for our kind, or else it is so old that it has faded close to nothingness. It will grow stronger as we climb—close your mind."

Sarita might close her mind, but she kept a tight grip on the awl. *"Lady—"* she said in a whisper of appeal. However, when Rhys started once more to lead Lopear on and she heard him talking soothingly to Valoris, she did not refuse to follow but trudged doggedly on. There was nothing else to do.

That night's camp was made in a narrow crevice between two rocks sprouting from the mountain cliff. The animals were staked out to browse as the rain had thinned to a mist. The three of them huddled together against the sharpness of the mountain wind and ate sparingly of their dwindling provisions.

When Sarita settled Valoris for the night, she wished she had at least a chance to provide the child with warm and dry clothing. This was summer, but treacherous chills could be caught as easily as in winter, and she would be lost if Valoris ailed, she knew so little of healing lore.

As she cuddled him closely, hoping some of the warmth of her own body might reach him, he whimpered, "Go home—" before he burrowed his face into her shoulder.

"How I wish that you could, little one," she whispered. She had been careful to dig the awl into a small crevice of the rock beside her so that its silver knob touched her own head. This uncanny place might well be an open door for what she feared the most.

Rhys asked no questions when he saw her action. Instead he opened his belt pouch to draw out two coins, newly minted by their shine. Into each a ragged edged hole had been bored, and through those he now knotted a bowstring.

When he was done, he held one of them out to the girl and looped the other over his neck. "Many men believe in the power of amulets," he said. "These are silver—by all lore, opposed to that which is friendly with the Dark. Perhaps they can give us armor of a sort."

If it was armor it did not hold against dreams. Sarita awoke at the dawn's first light and sat up, her cheeks wet with tears. She could not remember the substance of her dreams, only that they left her with a burden of sorrow and a sense of great loss. So great was her sorrow that she picked up Valoris and hugged him tightly while her gaze moved to the man just rousing himself from sleep.

"It— I do not know, yet I cry as if from some great hurt."

"It is old, I think. We, too, have seen and felt great hurts and therefore we are open to such pain. Yet—we must go on."

Sarita was ready to protest, but discovered that she could not. Fear seemed to have fled, what was left was a need to do just as he said. Still, as she reached for the awl, she was sure this was no compulsion leading her to follow some dark will. Rather it was like offering quiet respect—attending the funeral bier of someone much mourned.

Nor did that feeling leave her as the morning wore on and they climbed the faint trail. This was clearly the remains of a roadway, and at intervals along it were tall rocks set up on end like those which formed the circles. Yet if they had ever borne any inscriptions, time had long since worn them away.

Rhys came as a rear guard now. The animals displayed no signs of uneasiness, Berry snatching mouthfuls of coarse grass and low-growing bushes as she moved along. There were no trees on this height, though through the morning mists Sarita could see some on neighboring slopes.

13.

The way they followed became a series of broad ledges like giant steps. At least the rain had stopped, and as they reached the tenth of those great steps, the sun broke through, bathing them with light and warmth. There they paused long enough for Sarita to unwind Valoris' damp covering.

He no longer whimpered, in fact he was too quiet. If he fell into a fever, how could she manage? For the moment he seemed able to keep his seat on Lopear, though she watched him anxiously.

This strange stair wound around the side of LodenKail. Already they had lost sight of the land through which they had come. All there was to be seen were mountains nearly completely covered by dark, forbidding forests except for peaks bare to sun and wind.

The rock posts still marked the trail and Sarita had an impulse to hurry by each as it appeared. They made another turn and were now on the western slope of the mountain. Here the ledges stopped at the mouth of a shadowed crevice which appeared to be a door into the very heart of the mountain.

To go in there—Sarita shrank from the thought, but there was no turning back. Here the last and tallest of the pillars had been set, one on each side of that dark mouth. These bore what might have once been heads, but the features were too weather worn to tell.

There was no hint of evil here, only sorrow. Sarita felt moisture gather in her eyes, Valoris broke the silence with a cry, his hands up, hiding his face, as if he did not want to see what lay around him now.

Quickly the girl loosed him from his seat. He was crying now, not loudly, but with the low wail of a lost and miserable child.

"On!" Rhys came up, herding the rest of the animals so she had to give way and enter the crevice. Luckily it was no tunnel. Over their heads the summer sky still showed, but only rock walls rose starkly on either side. Nor was the passage long.

Sarita emerged with Valoris and looked down and about her. There were tales of how in the far past mountains had belched forth fire and the very stuff of their making, which had become molten. Was that what had happened here?

They stood at the top of a slope, rather steep to be sure, but one which could be descended. Below was a bowl of valley. The tough greenery which had framed the outer trail changed to lush growth; there were even trees of respectable size. To one side the smooth mirror of a lake reflected back the sky.

There appeared to be no other break in the bowl's walls—they must have come through the only passage.

"A pass—such as Felspar!" There was an excited note in Rhys' voice. "We shall have only one door to be guarded."

Had they indeed found a safe refuge? Sarita sighed and Valoris whimpered again. Well enough, but the child must be speedily cared for.

"Come." Her voice was curt. "I must get him out of these damp clothes. In fact, we had all better do that—lung fever comes not only in winter."

Their four-footed companions had already decided what was best for them. The goats were scrambling nimbly downslope, Lopear and Mouse behind. But Sarita, now weighted with Valoris, had to move much more slowly with Rhys' aid.

Once she was safe on the valley floor, the ranger quickly left her. He worked with deftness and erected a lean-to, the final roofing the waterproofed covering of their packs. Sarita trudged down to the lake, where the sun had warmed some flat rocks.

Once freed of his damp and sticky clothing and given a handful of dried plums, Valoris squatted on one of the reddish stones while the sun toasted him. At first he was content to just sit there peacefully. Then he crept over to the edge from which he could watch the water and began calling for Sarita to come and see the fish.

When they were ready to eat, Rhys returned from the lake with five of those fish strung on a tough reed, ready to be broiled over a fire he had no hesitation in lighting. Sarita gathered up the clothing they had changed out of and washed it, spreading the pieces out on the rocks to dry. She kept determinedly busy, for there was a kind of prickling—that was the only word she could think of to describe the feeling that they were only here by sufferance and what seemed a good place might still be a trap. From time to time she watched Rhys; he certainly showed no sign that he felt any of the warning or uneasiness he had spoken of.

When night came they ate again and made their beds in grass nests.

With sun-warmed and dried blankets, Sarita found it hard to keep awake. Little by little the tensions of the past days were leaving her, but it left a weariness which made it difficult even to raise her hand.

She crept in beside Valoris, knowing she could no longer fight her exhaustion. If there were to be any guards this night, was her last dull thought, the animals would have to provide them—Rhys was already rolled in his own blanket.

When she roused at last, the sun was up and there was no weight beside her. Valoris had crawled away.

Sarita sat up abruptly. It would seem that Rhys had also slept late, for she could see his covered form still on the other side of the fire, having chosen to leave the lean-to for her and the child.

She got to her knees, her uneasiness growing. Not too far away the donkeys and the goats were grazing, then Berry threw up her head and trotted toward the lake. But Valoris, always drawn to the company of the animals, was not to be seen.

The lake—the fish—!

Sarita was on her feet instantly, remembering his interest in the fish, and she ran toward the water, not stopping to put on her boots, her much-mended chemise flapping. Nor did she heed the rasp of the rocks on her bare feet as she crossed to the water's edge, where Valoris had been yesterday, fascinated by the water life below.

"Valoris!" she screamed, forcing herself to look down at the placid, reflective surface. Ripples raised by a light wind ran across it, but she could still see the sandy bottom. There was no small body there. She jumped in all the same, gasping at the chill. It was shallow enough, but she knew that to search the entire lake was beyond her power.

"Valoris!"

"What's to do?"

Rhys stood on the rocks from which she had just leaped, only short underdrawers covering his slim body. Then in a moment he, too, was in the water, his hand out to steady her when she slipped on a stone.

"I woke—" somehow she choked out the words "—he was gone! Yesterday he saw the fish—he might—"

The ranger made no answer, save to pull her ashore. His voice was curt and she cringed. "You cannot be sure of that, Sarita. Do not think of the worst before it is proven."

She dragged and screamed at him as he pulled her back to camp. He shook her so fiercely that her head wobbled on her neck.

"Be quiet—you waste breath for nothing! Let us see what is to be done."

He let go of her so suddenly she crumpled to the ground.

"Clothe yourself," he ordered. "You cannot go searching nearly bare."

She looked down at her body and flushed, but it was no time for modesty. Valoris was the important one. She began to dress as Rhys had commanded. The ranger had already thrown on his own clothing.

He did not wait for her, instead he was circling slowly about the now dead fire, eyes intent upon the ground. Sarita realized he was searching for a trail.

Suddenly the ranger swung away to where Lopear now grazed and Sarita followed him. There was a strip of ground where a tuft of grass had been vigorously pulled from its roots. Valoris!

He always went to Lopear the first thing in the morning with some grass he had pulled, the donkey receiving it gravely, as if they performed some private rite.

So he had fed Lopear—but there was still the lake and the fascinating fish!

Only Rhys was not heading in that direction. He went down on one knee, and she crowded closer to see what had caught his attention. There was another bare spot, a small depression as if something had been picked up—a stone moved. Valoris had always been fascinated by her sling and at times he had brought her stones he thought would be good ammunition.

Rhys sat back on his heels. He was plainly studying the stretch of ground before him as a scholar would worry out the meaning of a page of ancient, crabbed writing.

"Come." He did not wait to see if she were following. He did not need to—Sarita was treading on his very heels.

There was a flutter of rag from a thorny bush. Berries hung plump and purple all around and Sarita could now see the signs of harvesting quite well. There was also damp earth here and the print of a small foot was very clear.

"Valoris!" She put into that call all the authority she could, but no small voice piped in return.

Rhys cast ahead. To her ever growing hope the trail did not lead lakeward, but instead to the rock wall of the valley.

Here was the head of a brilliantly blue flower which had been plucked and then dropped. Rhys was down on his knees again by a pile of rocks directly against the cliff. He began picking up stones, tossing them to one side. What had been a small hole was rapidly being uncovered to show a wide opening. Valoris had crawled in *there*? But he did not like the dark. Why—?

Rhys had a space large enough to enter on hands and knees and she did not hesitate to follow him. Beyond that opening they could stand erect, and Sarita, looking about her, gasped.

This place was not hidden in darkness. Along the rock wall on either side curled and curved lines of a strange bluish light which, when she peered closer, she saw must rise from veins of crystal.

They stood at the mouth of what must be a tunnel. Rhys pointed to the floor beneath their boots. Earth and dust had shifted, but Valoris' prints were plain to see. Sarita opened her mouth to call the child's name—only to have Rhys stop her.

Ahead she could make out dim objects lying on the floor in a clutter. Stones fallen from above? Was Valoris following a dangerous path?

At the same moment she knew why Rhys had denied her call. The uneasiness she had felt ever since she had set foot on the way

up LodenKail was growing stronger. It was not fear of dark evil—
no, just that they were venturing into a place which was not for
their kind.

Rhys took a quick step to the left, but did not avoid kicking a
partly rounded object. It skittered sidewise to strike against the wall
and slew about.

Sarita gasped. She was looking down at a crumbling skull half
encased in the rusted remains of a helm—a crested helm. That crest
drew her eyes away from the skull itself. What had been fashioned
to crouch there, still unmarked by time, was a monster—an exact
copy of the one she had seen in the Fane at Raganfors!

She made a wide detour and stepped squarely on the blade of
a sword, so rusty that it went to brown flakes under her tread. Rhys
leaned closer to study the skull, but it did not touch it.

His mouth was set grimly as he said, as if attempting to reassure
himself, "Long dead."

Sarita caught at the ranger's arm. "The Loden—is that the sign
of the Loden?"

She did not wait for an answer but plunged ahead. There was
more clutter of broken weapons, of splintered and crumbling bones,
but still she was able to see Valoris' prints. A stray thought crossed
her mind. It was unlike the boy that he had not been attracted to
any of this debris. Instead it seemed he was hunting something
more interesting.

The *thing*—that which had summoned her! Was it lying in wait
ahead, now summoning its desired prey?

Sarita began to run. There seemed to be more light ahead. She
could hear the noise of Rhy's heels crunching the debris behind
her. Then he was shoulder to shoulder with her—

There were more clear signs of battle here. Sarita's throat ached
with the need to call for the child. But—if the child were under a
compulsion such as she had felt, he would not answer.

More light—together they burst out into a large cavern which
held them still for a second in sheer amazement. Here the crystal
lines were much wider. Though their light was wan and eerie, still
it made visible all that was there.

Directly before them was a level space and entangled there a gruesome mass in which one could not separate the bones of one of the dead from that of his neighbor, they were so tossed and twisted.

Cutting through this was a path clear and straight, its substance made of the blue crystals, looking almost like a stretch of ice.

This led directly to a dais centered in this hidden domain. Stretched on that was something which gleamed pale blue and pearly white, with rainbow hues running across it. By this crouched Valoris. He was running his hands back and forth along the shimmering stuff, and under his touch it gleamed clearer and brighter.

14.

"Pretty—pretty!"

Sarita dashed forward up the two steps to the dais and caught the child, holding him tightly although he squirmed and fought, howling with some of his old temper.

"Want—pretty—" He tried to push himself out of her hold.

He was all right—safe, not hurt, not at the bottom of the lake—that was all she could think of at the present.

Kicking, he broke her hold and scrambled on hands and knees back to his treasure.

"Pretty!"

At first the girl thought that what lay there was a long, wide strip of cloth. But cloth was not patterned with scales. . . . Her eyes swept along that length and then—

With a gasp she tried to seize Valoris again, but he scuttled out of reach. That—that was a head! She could trace eyeholes, a snout. But it all lay as flat as if only skin remained, no bones—no flesh.

Rhys was already past her. Drawing his sword he inserted its tip into a wide hole which might have been the mouth, lifting it up. It came easily as if it had no more weight than the cloth she had first thought it.

"Skin—it is only a cast skin. Snakes do so once a year."

"The skin of what?" Sarita demanded. "And if this is a shed skin—what of the owner?"

A puff of dust rose as the head slipped from the sword tip, setting them all coughing.

"Long gone. Sarita—this must be what if left of the Loden!"

"Pretty." Valoris was running his hand up and down on the scaled surface, which gleamed ever the brighter as he wiped the dust from it.

"Pretty!" Sarita commented sharply, and then realized that the child was right. She had seen purses and belts made of snake skin that brought high prices in Raganfors. But this far outshone anything of that kind. The Loden?

Rhys walked along the outstretched length, measuring it in paces. "It was almost two men tall," he commented, and then looked at the battleground below, "and it gave good account of itself. Look here." He knelt and pulled to straighten out what could only be a foreleg. At its tip were holes in a curved pattern of five. "Claws," he commented.

"But—" Sarita looked from the carnage below to the skin. If the creature had survived the battle and shed its skin, where had it gone? Though all that dust was a reassurance that a long time had passed.

"Perhaps it did not like to have its home invaded." Rhys actually smiled. "It went to leave the mess our kind made well behind it— long ago."

Valoris held up the paw Rhys had straightened out. "Pretty!"

Sarita did not hear him, for at that moment she was caught up again in that vast, overwhelming sorrow which had touched her before but now completely enfolded her. She stared at Rhys. There was a glitter in his eyes and he brushed his hand across them.

"This is more than a place of the long dead." He seemed to be picking and choosing words with care. "There was evil here, but it failed." She saw his hand go out tentatively to the skin as if to soothe some ancient pain.

"I do not think this creature was of the Dark," he continued, "no matter what legend says of it. It was a *man* who bore that monster on his helm."

The feeling of loss and pain was draining from Sarita. She, too, touched the skin. To her surprise it did not feel rough in spite of the visible scales. And her love for beauty, in no matter what shape, awoke. She knew of no weaver, no embroideress, who could produce such glory as this.

"Pretty." Valoris was looking up into her face.

"Yes," she agreed, "it is pretty."

Still she wanted out of there, that place of death where darkness stained the light. There was no fear left, only a rising disgust. She also wondered what manner of man in those long years past had chosen the monster as his symbol. Had they come to slay the Loden? Somehow she was sure they had not succeeded, the discarded skin appeared to answer that. Where the beast had gone—perhaps it was best not to question.

On impulse she worked the awl out of her belt and touched its silver knob to the skin. There was a flash, and as she jerked away she saw a tinge of the rainbow light wrap around the knob, appear to sink into it. And at that moment she was sure that Valoris had been led for some important reason to bring them here.

They had difficulty prying the boy from his find, but Sarita wanted him safely out of there, away from the tangle of rusted weapons. When he would not listen to her, Rhys swung him up in a strong grasp, nor did the ranger pay any attention to his screams of rage.

Once they were outside Rhys returned the screaming, struggling boy to Sarita and went to the business of again moving stones. This time he sealed the fissure past any ability of Valoris to reopen it. However, once more outside the child ceased his raging. Instead he made straight for the berry bushes and began cramming the fruit into his mouth with both hands.

They joined him, then moved slowly toward their camp. Sarita drew a deep and thankful breath. Her fear of the lake, and that pall of sorrow which had fallen over her inside the cavern, had left her weary.

As she took Valoris' hand, he came willingly enough until he caught a glimpse of Briar and pulled free to run to the kid.

Busying herself with camp duties the girl continued to keep an eye on him, but he showed no sign of wandering off again. Rhys came up, bow shouldered, with Lopear's hackamore in one hand.

"Yesterday I saw osdeer tracks." He was so much his usual self that she could almost believe what just lay behind them was some kind of dream. "You will be safe enough."

Instinctively she knew he was right. In spite of what lay hidden in the walls which bordered it, the valley was safe. And they needed food. An osdeer would mean hide to patch boots already wearing thin.

It was past noon before Sarita finished the overhaul and washing of all their spare clothing. Valoris, worn out at last, curled up on a blanket and went to sleep as she hummed softly in time to her sewing.

Sewing rooms were never places of quiet. While apprentices were not permitted to chatter freely, there were intervals when Dame Argalas set one of the seniors to reading an edifying book aloud from the guildhouse library. And often they had sung.

Sarita thought of that other life—for it *had* been another life, as if death had found her at Var-The-Outer and issued her into another existence. She tried to reckon up the days since the taking of the keep and could not be sure of her tally.

The best she could figure was that there had been at least five or six ten-days. So long! These days had slid into each other, marked only by the need to prepare food, mend clothing, and tramp in the wilderness. If they could only have stayed at the lodge! The lean-to behind her now was a very poor exchange for what she now looked back upon as luxury.

If they were to stay here long, they would need better housing. There were not enough trees for building, nor had they the proper tools for such labor. Unwillingly she remembered that cavern to which she resolutely kept her back as she worked. To live there! She could not face clearing out that debris of death—certainly it was a place of ill omen. Where, then?

Sarita got to her feet to stretch, having carefully fitted her bone needle into the padded case. Slowly she turned, surveying all she could see of the valley.

It might be nearly the size of one of the large valley farms. The wildlife here was limited and Rhys had decreed early that they would not hunt the leapers or grass hens for the pot unless circumstances forced them to it.

At least the land was open enough so that they had been able to know from the first there were no larger beasts, except those they had brought with them. But now her eyes caught an irregularity near where Berry grazed. A rock protruding? Sarita shaded her eyes against the sun's glare. It was more than just a rock, she decided, and it abutted the valley cliff. Her curiosity stirred. She wanted no more surprises.

Valoris sat up and favored her with a wide grin: another tooth was appearing. Sarita laughed.

"Little lord, you are in a hurry to grow. Now let us go and see what Berry has found—"

With his hand in hers, Sarita plowed through the ragged clumps of grass. Valoris wriggled free and made a grab for a large black hopping insect, the biggest Sarita had ever seen, which took to the air with a powerful thrust of its hind legs. Briar came bleating to join them as they neared his mother.

Sarita stopped short. She had been right in her suspicions—that was no natural ledge of rock. Stone it was, but sat perfectly square, and the blocks which formed it were fitted together with such precision she could hardly distinguish the lines between one block and the next.

She loosed her mind touch—did any peril rest there? But she felt nothing. Valoris ran ahead to hug Berry, but Sarita now passed beyond the child. Those block walls were nearly the height of her shoulder, and as she walked around them she could find no opening. Yet it had been obviously erected for a purpose. It was a square, nearly the size of the lodge.

On impulse Sarita caught the top edge and pulled herself up. Here, too, was a platform of blocks with an unbroken surface—or was it? An eye used to catching flaws in a fabric centered on the middle of the surface.

Sarita strode toward that, realizing that the texture of the stones changed there. Though they were all still a dull gray, there was a difference. She dropped to her knees and ran her fingertips over the area. Where the other stones were rough, this one had a slick surface. Yet to the eye it still looked rough.

Sarita drew the awl and put its point down on one of the lines marking that different square. The meeting of metal with the surface gave forth a ringing sound. Quickly she moved to outline the full block.

It was when she reached the fourth side that the awl point no longer ran smoothly but caught. Another clear, ringing sound sent her scrambling away from the square. It began to move, rising upward perhaps a handsbreath—a trapdoor!

Before she could move it fell back once more into place. Perhaps she could have prevented that closing. However—no, she would wait for Rhys' return before trying any more experiments. She had no wish to be trapped.

Putting away the awl, Sarita crossed the platform she now believed to be a roof and swung down to Valoris. Mouse had moved to join them as if he felt the need for company with his comrade gone for the day.

Again the girl made a slow circuit of the walls, this time running her fingertips along the stone. There were no more slick blocks. When Rhys returned they must certainly make sure of this place, discover if it offered any danger.

Curiosity led to impatience as the afternoon wore on. She had hoped he would be back by dusk, but at last she laid a small fire fed by dead branches of berry bush. Wood for a fire might be a problem also. Would they have to bring it in from some distance?

It was close to true dark, and she had already fed Valoris and settled him in his blanket nest, when she heard the bray she recognized as Lopear's.

There was no osdeer on the donkey, but a bundle of leapers, gutted and ready to be skinned, and two larger animals that resembled leapers but were longer of leg. Rhys dropped the smelly load and led Lopear aside to wipe down the donkey's back with a fistful of grass before loosing the beast.

Though it was never a task she relished, Sarita was busy with the carcasses. They must be dealt with quickly before the meat could spoil.

She had skinned two of the small leapers and had them spitted by the fire before Rhys returned. The smell of slightly scorched meat no longer bothered her, rather, it stimulated her appetite.

"Good hunting," she commented.

Rhys made a sound close to a grunt. There was a suggestion of a stoop to his shoulders as if he might have traveled far.

"Creature hereabouts have not been hunted," he commented. "There is no sign that anyone has come this way—at least—" he paused as if remembering the dead in the cavern "—for a long time."

"There is something here." Sarita stopped work for a moment.

He was instantly alert, the signs of fatigue vanishing. "What have you found?"

She reported her visit to the place of stones as quickly but as accurately as she could. He was listening closely.

"You had no warning?" he asked swiftly.

Sarita shook her head. "I—I tried. There was nothing to be felt."

"Hmmm." His busy hands had ceased work and he looked off into the thickening night.

"Tomorrow we shall see," he said a second later.

But after they had eaten and Sarita had done all she could to preserve his kills, she watched him from where she lay beside Valoris. He did not seek out his own bedroll but rather stood for a long time facing out into the dark. She guessed what he was doing— putting his talent to work, even as she had earlier done.

15.

Once more Sarita stood in the great hall of the keep, before her the dais with its seats of honor. One of those was now centered and in it crouched a figure which seemed to be shriveled, drawn in upon itself, as she had seen insects shrivel too near a candle flame. There was nothing imposing or awesome about he who played lord here.

However, that gray shadow figure towered, its presence far more to be felt than the shriveled man to which it played mock deference as it stood beside him. It seemed to Sarita that she could see a spouting of words—if one could *see* words—which the Gray One was using as both a leash and a lash to keep its prey under control.

Sanghail had his master now beside him, and it was from that master that the cold evil spread. The head and face of that dark sentinel were still hidden under a hood, and Sarita found it good that that was so—she did not want to see what was concealed.

All of a sudden the Gray One swung about, away from the chair in which cowered its companion. A skeleton-thin hand arose, and in its palm there burned, with a sullen flame, a carving of the monster's head.

She swayed. The very sight of that had been like a foul blow. She swayed, but did not yield. The Gray One took a step forward. She could sense a rising rage. Was she really in the hall? Had somehow that summons brought her over leagues to stand captive before these two? So clear was all which lay about her that she almost believed she was there.

"Serpent spawn!" The words were hissed at her, and again she

102

was able to see them as well as hear; they were darkly red, like old blood.

That hand appeared to stretch farther and farther toward her as if the arm behind it was unnaturally elongated. And the carrion stench of what it held was thick in her throat.

"Be—not!" ordered that hissing voice.

Still, what had brought her here held and she stood firm. The Gray One advanced now to the very edge of the dais. Its outheld arm swept through the air as if it meant to throw the abomination at her.

"I am!" somehow the words had come to her lips. And she could see those also, bright sparks cutting through the gathering gloom.

"Be—not!" That was a harsh scream of rage, and now the black carving was thrown at her in truth.

The hall was gone. She stood, but in another place. Here there was no stifling dark, but rather a soft glow of pearly light. However, she could not see more than was immediately around her. There was a depression in the floor at her feet, and in it rested a white, egg-shaped object across which played a constant coil and recoil of many colors, as if it were a giant gem.

She was but a puppet for the use of that which had brought her here, for now her hands arose without any violation on her part and she stooped to lay both of them palm flat against the ovoid. Into her flowed energy. Her mind reeled—there was too much to be absorbed all at once. She cried out in pain.

"Sarita!"

Very faintly through the muddle in her mind the voice reached her. Still she could not break contact with the object. It was her master—even as the Gray One had mastered Sanghail—yet also she dimly knew that this was no source of evil.

"Sarita!"

Her hands fell away from what she touched. The light was gone, like a snuffed candle. Though her mind was still awhirl, she was now aware of something else: she half lay in another's arms, and there was a growing frantic note in that summoning voice:

"Sarita!"

The girl opened her eyes. It was dark, but not the Dark that had crept out from the walls of the great hall—this was the honest dark of night. She felt leather against her cheek, smelled wood smoke, and looked up into the face now leaning down close to hers.

"Rhys?"

The switch from dream world to real dazed her, but not enough that she could miss the fear in his expression, lit as it was by the last glow of their dying fire.

"What—what had you?" His tight hold eased as he realized that she was once more aware.

"I—I don't know—" Her mouth was suddenly dry and the fear which had gripped her when she had stood before the Gray One seemed to crash down on her in a single blow. Then that other presence stirred from where it had coiled inside her—that which had filled her in the place of light.

"It—it was not a dream!" With sudden energy she freed herself from his hold and sat up, staring wide-eyed into the dark. No, whatever had happened to her had been no dream. She was—changed. Just how and why she did not yet know.

"What did you see?" His voice was ragged, as if he had been pushed to some inner limit of his own.

Slowly, with pauses between the words as she tried to remember each detail, Sarita answered him.

"What does Sanghail deal with?" he blurted out when she had finished.

"I think," and her scrambling of new knowledge told her that she spoke the truth, "nothing of our own world. Something more powerful and older." She shivered.

He moved swiftly and drew a blanket about her shoulders. "There is far more in this than an envy-inspired strike against the earl. But—it could not command you!" His arm still lay across her shoulders, holding the blanket in place.

"Rhys—that place—we must go there!" Just as the Gray One had laid a compulsion upon her, so now Sarita felt a pull.

"It's near dawn," he answered. "At first light we will go, but first let us eat. And you are shivering—come closer—" He urged her to the fire pit and built up the blaze again.

There was a sleepy sound from Valoris. Then the child came to her also. Sarita pulled him under her blanket cloak. She tried to concentrate on what was immediately around her and so keep all those strange whirling thoughts at bay.

"There comes a battle—" Sarita said suddenly. Of that she was certain. Rhys tensed.

"When—and where?" His demands were fast and harsh.

But she could only shake her head. "I do not know ..." she admitted, allowing her answer to trail forlornly away.

Dawn grayed the sky, but as yet there was no sight of the sun. They ate, Sarita making herself choke down her portion of food.

Rhys sat watching her. That she had faced some great ordeal this past night was not to be denied. Had he not already believed in talents beyond the definition of men, he would have said that she had had only a disturbing dream, but he was sure that more was at stake.

As they set off across the meadow toward the strange block of fitted stones, he carried his sword, though certainly what Sarita had faced in the night could not be deterred by any blade. The feeling of strangeness was growing stronger in him, and he set Valoris down from his shoulders and used Sarita's old trick of harness and leash to make sure the child would not stray nor try to follow them.

Once on the top of the square structure Sarita pointed out the trapdoor. However, Rhys' knife point could find no entrance into the lines she had traced yesterday. He sat back on his heels, surveying the obstinate stone.

Sarita had not spoken since they had left the camp, moving with a definite purpose in view, uncaring that she was accompanied. Now she looked down at him as if she really saw him for the first time.

"The awl—it was the awl!"

In a moment she was beside him, the point of the small tool set to the crack. Once more she traced carefully around the square and again there came a sharp, high sound and the block rose. This time Rhys moved, catching the edge of the door, adding his strength to send it all the way back.

They looked down. There was no darkness, rather a gleam of light which came from no source unless it was from the walls. Immediately beneath was a circular space like a shallow well. From this,

equally distant, were four openings, and by one a fifth and narrower way.

Here was no smell of mustiness, no sign of dust. This might
have been swept clean to prepare for their coming. After a moment
of hesitation Rhys swung over the edge and made a short drop to
the floor. Sarita wasted no time in following him.

Once her feet touched the smooth surface the girl knew where
she stood—and why also began to form into a distinct order.

"Is—this is the birthing center!" The turmoil of knowledge
began to strengthen in her mind. "These are the egg chambers."
She turned abruptly into the nearer of the doorways; the walls wid-
ened out in a curved pattern which met at a point at the far end,
so that the low chamber was like a flower petal in design.

There was a depression in the floor half filled with a glitter of
dust. Sarita gave a low cry.

"Gone!"

She pushed past Rhys and made for the next chamber, and the
next, only to make the same discovery. The sense of loss which she
had felt in the cavern with the Loden's skin was now weighing so
heavily upon her that her breath came in sobs.

The last chamber! She sank to her knees beside that depression.
No dust! No—fitted closely into that was an ovoid shape such as
she had seen and touched in her night vision. But she did not
venture to touch this one—she feared it was too fragile, that it would
shatter into dust as had the others.

Rhys knelt beside her. The ranger was staring at the egg as he
might at some creature which was removed from all forms of nature
he knew. His sword was laid aside; slowly his hand came forth
toward that opal-tinted curve of shell.

"No!" Sarita cried out in protest. Then the undigested knowledge took her over. Just as she had known this wonder in a vision,
so now he needed to do likewise.

His brown, calloused hand curled about the swell of the egg
near the top of its curve. The girl saw him stiffen, his body jerk
back, but not far enough for him to lose contact.

There was pain screwing up his features, beads of sweat formed
along the edges of his face—he was a man being stretched to the
limit of endurance.

"No—" his faltering voice was a whisper "—no—too much!"

Yet he did not move. Now Sarita put her own hand on his shoulder. She could feel a subtle shaking of his body which she could not see. But she continued to hold him, even as he had held her. Then at last his hand fell limply, away from the egg as if his wound had reopened, and he turned to look at her.

"It—what has it done to me?"

"To us," she said quietly.

"Our kind are not meant for—for—"

"Such knowledge." She found the words he sought. "No, but it is now ours to bear."

"Yet that which was to be born of this—" he pointed to the egg "—is dead."

"In body," the girl conceded. "However, perhaps the purpose for which it was conceived had not yet been faced. Thus what it knew was saved—until there was a need."

"The Loden—" he said wonderingly.

"It was guardian for this land, only those who dealt evily needed to fear it. But it is long gone. This was its last gift to those it shielded."

"I saw—the earl—fighting in the city—the Gray One possessing the people."

So the egg had played prophet for him? There was undoubtedly a reason for that also.

"We have been given a weapon—weapons—"

Rhys nodded. "But—" both of his hands flew up to either side of his head "—too much all at once. Time to think—"

"That will be given us also, I believe." Inwardly she felt as uncertain and adrift as he must at this moment. There was a clutter of impressions she must sort out. Strange sentences which must be part of incantations of another time, even of another race, would be clear for an instant or two and then fade again. Yes, they needed time to think.

She looked down at the egg. She almost had expected it to crumble into dust as had its fellows after it had given its knowledge to Rhys, but it seemed to be firm and solid.

On sudden impulse, doubtless moved by one of the floating bits of knowledge, she, in turn, leaned forward to touch it. As she did so, in her mind was a clear picture of Dame Argalas as she had seen her last, riding on her mule with the earl's retinue.

Above where her fingertips lay on the egg, the ever-moving shimmer of the rainbow lights vanished. She might be looking through a small window, so clear was what lay before her—she felt she could have reached through and touched the guild mistress. But this was not the Dame Argalas Sarita had known for so many years; this blank-eyed woman crouched on matted straw in a stone-walled hole.

Rhys must have shared her vision, for he drew a deep breath. "Imprisoned—your mistress imprisoned! What—"

"Worse—much worse—" Sarita was following her own line of thought. The scene of Dame Argalas had winked out as she released the concentration which held it. "But, Rhys—see you—we have that which can give us sight of our enemies!"

His face was suddenly transformed, though the grin his lips shaped was like a wolf's snarl.

"That we can, that we can!"

16.

When they came out of the egg chamber Sarita turned to the narrower opening beside it. There was still more that they must see—or perhaps do. The passage beyond was narrow, so she led the way, Rhys following. There were stairs before them and they climbed.

Those gave upon a wide anteroom with a half-circle of doorways. Rhys, now matching step with Sarita, headed directly to the one facing the head of the stairs. So they came together into the Audience Chamber—the Hall of Judgment Eternal—for both of them knew what this was.

Together they stood before a dais similar to the one they had seen in the Loden cavern. In the center was a long, raised section from which rays of light shone: blue, white, tinged now and then with a hint of rainbow. To the right of that was a tall-backed chair— a throne, in truth.

The throne was crystal clear, save for a silver inlay on the back— a four-petaled flower.

"The Blossoms of Grace," Sarita said slowly. How many times had she seen that design reproduced—always on any banner or offering meant for the Lady.

However, Rhys had turned his head a little to stare at the other side of the dais. There had certainly once been another chair, but what remained had been half-melted, as metal is reduced by fierce fire.

Seemingly of itself his sword rose and pointed to that mass of fused stone or metal.

"Traitor, Death in Life—" The words exploded from the ranger as mighty oaths. "So again the battle! Rathban that was—Rathban that seeks to live again!"

His call awakened something—something very old, but not broken by either time or the force of light which had driven it into the outer darkness from which it struggled now to return. A curl of reddish smoke reached out, pointing to his outstretched sword.

Sarita cried out, but Rhys already understood the peril. He forced the sword down with effort, and as he did so also shouted:

"Not for your plucking, your arming, Rathban. By the Will of the Scaled One, by the Will of the Lady, we stand upon the other side—keep to your dark, double-tongued, ours is the Light!" His words rang in an invocation.

The smoke curled and recurled, as if some pressure was forcing it back into the dark debris from which it had risen. The great seat of the Loden might be bare of the once-shining body in its glory, the Lady might no longer hold court here, but what they had meant, had been—no—were!—remained the same now and forever.

But what would be the task laid upon those standing there now? As yet they were not sure, only that there was that which they must do—be—and the time for knowing would soon be upon them.

There was an exultation in that thought, Sarita found. But one could not live on such a high plane. She blinked and blinked again, as if waking from sleep. Still, she knew well that there did rest within her now strengths she had never known she would have or could carry.

The audience was finished, if their confrontation with the dais and what stood there could be called that. Sarita found herself making as low a courtesy as she would to the High King, while Rhys brought his sword up in formal salute. They passed quickly out of the chamber, as if they now intruded.

However, they were not yet done exploring, and they went through each of those doors in the outer hall. What they discovered must have once been the living quarters of those chosen to serve the Great Ones. And here Sarita did not feel that they intruded, rather they they were being offered what they needed the most: safe and secure shelter.

Thus they moved from their rough camp into chambers which

had not known the fall of human feet in more generations than
Sarita believed could be counted. Nor were their new quarters mere
stone-walled barrows. Rather, cunningly set into the rock cliff in
which they were contained were slits of that substance which resembled stone and yet let through the light of day. There were also
hoops in the wall where torches might be placed.

Valoris took to his new home with the same absorbing interest
he had shown when drawn to the Loden skin. Yet he made no
move to enter the great hall. Sarita wondered once if the child
might be open to that which still clung about the destroyed throne
and had some geas laid upon him not to go near it.

Nor did either Sarita or Rhys seek out the chamber of the egg
again. By instinct they knew that the time was not yet right for that.
Though, as they talked together of an evening, they often compared
the vast, broken lines of thought which they remembered and felt
the need to make sense of.

It was plain to them now that there had once been a mighty
struggle—one that had ended first in the Loden cavern, and then—
without the aid of humankind—in the Audience Chamber. Three
powers had ruled until one sought to stand alone. Man had been
drawn into that tangle, and a bitter war had been fought which had
turned a good and fertile earth to a wasteland. But the dark power
had assumed too much, building upon the energy of human servants
until he was so thinned that he was open to what waited—and
struck.

That which was the inner core of his being, just as that which
was also the inner core of his former companions, could not be
totally destroyed. It withdrew to another place. Those of the Light
were also worn by the struggle, and they were lost to men's memories
save as legends of good forces to be called upon.

The evil which had tried to slay the Loden had cast its image
into human minds as a monster. And in one fashion that ancient
fear had kept safe what lay there.

They had been a number of days in that strange temple of the
Three—for a temple it was, holding treasures they discovered during
their explorations. Valoris played with an armload of small animals
fashioned of gold and gems; Sarita might have gone bejeweled as
an empress, if she wished. The beauty of the stones drew her, but

she was not tempted to wear them. Instead she awoke one morning with the full knowledge that she had been summoned for another duty.

Strange, she thought as she fingered the tools at her belt one by one. Why? No, that was not to be asked now—rather how and when. And when came first. Once they had eaten and Rhys had prepared to go out for a hunt, she stopped him.

"There is something I must do, and for it I need your help."

"That being?"

"The Loden skin—it must be brought forth—there is a use for it."

He stared at her in surprise. "What use—?"

She shook her head impatiently. "I know it only in part, but it is in here," she struck the palm of her hand against her forehead, "and it will come, but first I must have the skin."

So once more they made the journey to where he had closed the fissure, and she helped him pull away the rocks he had so carefully piled there. Valoris was with them, suddenly impatient, trying to squirm between their hands and slip in as soon as the hole was uncovered. Sarita had to stop and restrain him during the last moments of work.

They made a careful way through the place of the dead and came once more into the Loden's hall. Sarita looked around, noting now the stains which dulled some of the crystal veining—signs of ancient fire. They had drawn fire to their use, those last dark fighters. This had once been a place of glory and light. She would do what she must do, and then they would leave it to the shadows of the past forever.

She went directly to where the skin lay, Valoris running a little ahead. Once more he stroked the scaled length, but she pushed him back, brushing it over with a bunch of leafed twigs, freeing it from the dust of ages. Its glorious colors appeared to shine nearly as brightly as the wall veins of crystals.

When Sarita had cleaned it as best she could, she began to roll it—but this was a task in which she did need help. While the skin was as thin and supple as silk, there was so much of it that Rhys stepped in to aid her. In the end it took the two of them to balance the roll across their shoulders and bring it out of the place of death into the bright morning.

The three of them had no more than won free when there was a rumble behind them. Startled, Sarita loosed her hold on the skin and half turned. Those stones which had hidden the doorway were being added to by a shower of rocks from above. Rhys' hand closed upon her arm. He, too, dropped his portion of the skin to drag both the girl and the child away from the avalanche. That his was some whim of nature neither of them believed. So had the past of the Dark been sealed from the eyes of humankind.

Only the large hall before the Audience Chamber was large enough to again unroll the skin and stretch it flat. Sarita crawled along its length on her hands and knees, inspecting it with the critical attention which had been trained into her. The underparts were smoother, the scales more tightly interlocked. They were also paler in color, darkening on the back ridges. It was most deeply shaded about the head, which now lay outspread like a carnival mask. Having made as sure as she could of her materials, Sarita went for the measuring rod, which she had never set aside and forgotten during their wanderings.

"Valoris!" Her voice was a sharp summons, for the child who was patting the far end of the strong tail, which must have been part of a support for the Loden, as the forelimbs were unnaturally short in comparison. "Come here."

When he had obeyed, she used the measure first for height and then for breadth, noting the markings down on a small ivory tablet from her pouch. In addition to the rigid measure, she had a series of small cords knotted together, and now she shook these free and began to take the sizing of the boy's arms and legs.

Rhys had watched her in silence, but now he asked:

"What would you do?"

Sarita knotted the final cord to the proper size. She pushed hair back from her face.

"My art is called for now, Rhys. Now you!" With an impatient gesture she beckoned him to stand in Valoris' place and lifted the measuring rod once more.

"This skin—you would fashion—clothing—" He took a step away and there was a shadow of repulsion on his face.

"This was set on me, ranger!" she retorted. "Yes—I fashion body coverings for all of us, but it is more than clothing. Do guardsmen not wear armor? I have seen the earl go forth in full iron armor—"

"This skin is tissue—far from any armor!"

"Do not be sure of that. Stand still now—let me see."

Perhaps it was her certainty of tone which reduced him to obedience. He stood still and let her take measurements even as she had done for Valoris. When she had the notes inscribed on her tablet, she gave new orders:

"Now do this for me also."

He was awkward about the business, needing instructions to knot the sleeve strings correctly and be sure of the measures she could not make for herself.

At last they were done and she had two leaves of her ivory slip inscribed with the smallest writing she had been able to use in order to have it all recorded.

Then she drew a deep breath and began moving the measure along the skin itself, being careful of the rents and holes left when it had been shed. It would take expert cutting—she stopped to consult her notes several times—but she was certain it could be done. Except . . . She had never thought of that. Thread! Where was a thread tough enough and yet supple enough?

Something in her expression must have given away the sudden realization of what was lacking, for Rhys spoke again:

"What is your need?"

Sarita answered without turning to look at him. "Thread—there is no thread!"

He dropped down beside where she was crouched. "What kind of thread, seamstress?"

"Stout cording perhaps such as is used in horse trappings. I have the needle right enough." She pulled out her horn box and unrolled the length of material into which each of her treasures had been so carefully fitted.

"This I use for leather." She twirled the long, bone needle between her fingers. "I am sure it will serve, but with no thread it is useless."

"Wait." He scrambled to his feet and left her frowning at the skin and her tools, wondering what she could use to do what her night's dreaming had planted in her mind.

When he came back, he had a coil in his hands. "Bowstrings," he told her.

Amazement broke through Sarita's self-absorption. She knew what those strings meant to him and how much he depended upon them. But excellent as they were, they were not enough.

Then her hands flew to her hair and she clawed loose the ragged braid she had bound it into. Her fingers had served as a comb for many days, and now she jerked at tangles. But her hair was long, over her shoulders, nearly touching the pavement on which she now sat.

It would be like the old task—the one which had occupied her on that morning when she had seen the countess ride out of Var-The-Outer. Only this time she would not be dealing with gold leaf and a silken core but rather with hair and—

She picked up the bowstrings and nearly shook them in Rhys' face. "Can these be split?"

He took them from her. "Perhaps, Sarita, but what would waste such strength as they have."

"No!" She shook her head vigorously so that her hair flapped on the air. "Those—" She nodded at the bowstrings "—they will be the core. This—" she grabbed up a handful of what straggled about her shoulders and shook it "—will be the outer winding. It is my craft, Rhys. I know the fashioning of thread and this I can do!" Now she held up her head and brushed the loose hair back from her shoulders. "Cut—cut it all, as close to my head as you can."

He took her scissors and long strings of hair fell to the floor and across her knees while she held very still. She would need a spool frame, but somehow she did not doubt that she could find that also.

17.

Rhys slipped out of the way to the bowl valley and stood on the outer slopes of LodenKail. Though he kept to cover, he felt the kind of freedom which possessed him whenever he was out in the wilderness. He had not brought one of the donkeys this time. Instead he had no thought of hunting . . . for meat.

Though Sarita's compulsion to get the Loden skin and her apparent desire to work her craft upon it had taken up much of the morning, he had been plagued all along with that sense of danger to come. Now he lifted his head and drew in a deep breath as if he were some predator trying for a promising scent.

There it was— He moved cautiously from one bit of cover to the next. There was a stirring—nothing he could hear or see, but which only could be felt. Once in awhile he shook his head violently, trying to put into order fragments of that knowledge he had gained from the egg.

Yes—the Dark walked—rode—or crawled. Not here—not yet— but it was abroad. He had no idea what drove Sarita to her needlecraft; it seemed to him a vain employment for the here and now.

And had she really understood when he told her that he might be gone for more than a day—that he was driven by the need for a long scout?

It was already well into the afternoon; they had spent so much time with the retrieval of the skin and Sarita's measuring and planning. He had thought to be on his way a little after first light. Again he paused to listen, not only with his wilderness-trained ears but with his talent.

There! His head swung abruptly north as if pulled by a noose. North—he looked to landmarks he knew from earlier days and those he had learned later. There was the pass—and there were other ways, hidden and known mainly to lurking wolfheads. The Lookout—he had evidence enough that it had fallen into enemy hands. Yet it was north he was drawn, and he did not try to evade that pull.

The tantalizing thread which drew him brought him down LodenKail and into thick woods. At once he was aware of the curious silence. If anything feathered, four-footed, or two-footed walked there, it was done in stealth.

These trees were very old, their trunks mossy. He slipped among them, not even coming across a game path. Instead his boots sank a little into the mass of long fallen leaves and ferns.

The warning suddenly blazed high, as if it had been shouted in his ear. Rhys stopped short. There was more light than forest gloom ahead; he might well be coming to clearing or glade. Now he set himself to become a shadow among shadows, creeping forward with all the guile he had learned from childhood.

A tall stand of brush was a curtain before him. It was so thick and matted he knew he could not work his way through without considerable noise. But he was right, there was an open space ahead. Now he picked up the scent of a camp: fire, horses, the general rank odor left by humankind when they took no care of their surroundings.

Still the silence held. Rhys was emboldened to creep closer, so that at last he had an open view of the clearing. There were indeed men there—at one side a party of six wearing surcoats bearing Sanghail's badge. Before them was a motley gathering of what could only be wolfheads.

He could also dimly see a horse line far to one side. But there was no stir from either man or beast. They stood as if some winter storm had wrapped them around and frozen them into place—the eeriness of the scene heightened Rhys' sensation of the Dark at work.

Among the party, which must have come from the conquered keep, there was another—with no sign of armor or weapon about him. Rhys' full attention was drawn to the stark gray figure who was holding both hands high. Between their united fingertips balanced something black which seemed to swell and throb even as Rhys caught a glimpse of it.

No! His jumble of past knowledge brought an instant warning. *Do not look.* Somehow his eyes had already flinched away from that foul object.

However, these others ... Glancing from man to man, the ranger was sure that all were held spellbound by what the gray one held aloft. Mind binding!

Through that blanket of silence he began to hear a sound, more a rhythm carried by the air about him rather than any words.

Rhys stiffened as the pattern began to make sense. This gray horror was binding men, making them merely extensions of his own foulness. The ranger kept his eyes carefully away from the mind speaker, and he quickly shut out what he could of that distant pattern of a ritual once well forgotten in this land. However, when he looked from man to man again, he could see that some of their humanity had gone out of them, that they had been changed—

Without thinking why, his hands moved to the breast of his jerkin and his fingers closed about the silver coin he wore on a neck thong. It seemed to him that when he held it tightly in his fist, the undercurrent of sound-that-was-not-sound dwindled, dulled.

Or perhaps it was that the Gray One had come to the end of what he could do here. His bony hands flipped the blackness down and it disappeared into one of his wide sleeves.

The tall gray form appeared to shimmer, to lose substance, and was gone, while those gathered there in the clearing came to life as men awakened from a deep sleep. Though at first they moved sluggishly, they lost that bemused concentration which had changed each face into a mask.

One of the soldiers came forward. He wore a twist of red about his right arm and Rhys took him for the leader—at least of those from the castle. His voice rang out sharply:

"That thrice-damned Florian rides to war—upon us. We shall give him a hot welcome to throw him and his kind into the depths."

There was a murmur from those listening. Then one of the outlaws spoke up. He was a giant of a man, furred on his bared arms like a quadbear, yet there was no suggestion in his face that he was one slow of wit.

"There was a bargain, liegeman. Does that still hold?"

Among his own fellows there was now a louder murmur and one man, smaller, with a rat's sharp features and cunning well written about him, dared to catch at the giant's arm.

"We are not minded," his voice was as shrill as a rat's squeak, "to go against what had been ordered. Marken, no one spits in the eye with—that!" He was now looking beyond the other to where the Gray One had stood. "Do you seek to draw the black fire upon us?"

The murmur arose to a chorus of fierce assent. If Marken had not completely bowed to the will of the one giving the orders, then at least his fellow had. Yet the giant, with a sharp twist of his arm, sent the rat man sprawling away from him and half turned to face those behind him.

"Dark gods demand blood." His voice was a roar now. "How do we know that we have not been signed as sacrifices? Open fighting—that is for a man, yes. But to deal with demons—that is a chancy thing. I say we keep to our bargain made with your lord." Now he addressed the soldier. "We shall be paid as we were before, and we shall not be driven like bulls to the slaughter because some power your lord bows to will have it so. This land—" he flung out his arm in a gesture to encompass what stretched around him "—be ours by rights of holding, even as your lordling sits in his hall and looks upon his fields. This much I say now: give yourself to the Dark and there will be—"

Suddenly he clutched at his chest where hair showed through the rents of a dingy shirt under an unlaced jerkin. He gasped, wheezed, sank to his knees. In spite of the pain, his features were twisted into a mask of rage, which gave way to a cloud of despair as he sank forward and lay facedown.

The wolfhead crew shrank back. But the red-badged sergeant took a step forward. "Look you well," he commanded. "This one questioned—now what is he but a carcass? You have your orders—see that you follow them." With that he turned swiftly and, with the other liegemen, went to the horse lines where they speedily mounted and rode into the wood beyond. But the wolfheads remained where they were, nor did any of them venture to approach the fallen giant.

To Rhys' complete astonishment the body was stirring—the man had not been death-stricken after all! However, when he got first to his knees and then to his feet, his face was empty, as if nothing human now filled his body. Those of his kind edged away from him.

"They come against us on the twisted track." Even his deep voice had lost a touch of life; he might be repeating something another had said. "Forken!"

The rat man scuttled back as if to escape the attention of Marken. But he was speedily caught and held, though he twisted for freedom in the grip of two larger fellows.

"Forken, you have told us many times that you know more of these hills than even the rangers—and since they are now finished, your sneaking about will be put to the test."

Marken, his face still blank, advanced on the captive, who looked at the giant with fear and despair twisting his features.

Marken stood directly before him. He put out a heavy hand and slapped the smaller man with force enough to send the other's head against his shoulder. Had he not been in his captors' grip, it was plain that the blow would have smashed him to the ground.

"Forken—you will be our guide—"

Oddly enough all the wild fear the other had shown a moment before was wiped away and his narrow face was as void of emotion as Marken's.

"I lead," he said in a dull voice.

"You lead," Marken commented, as if to enforce the action suggested.

Rhys drew a deep breath. Whatever possessed Marken now also held Forken. Thus this compulsion could be passed from one to another even as a plague would spread down the streets of a city.

They busied themselves, collecting the gear which lay around their campsite and then, each man slinging a pack, they started north and west, the thing that had once been Marken in the lead.

For the moment Rhys could not move. What he had seen happen was against all belief, but the knowledge which had come to him in the valley of the Loden began to answer the questions his common sense demanded to have explained.

Yes, that power which the Dark served could strike the wits from a man, make him an empty body, able to fight, to serve, but with no life, no heart left in him—if the wolfheads had ever known such softer emotions. The liegemen had not shown that blankness of face; therefore, if they were mind bound, they were still human. Was that fact one which could be used to turn them against the sorcery of the Gray One? A glimmer of hope suggested that it was true.

However, he must follow them, must know of this so-called twisted path. Familiar as he was with the woods, he had never heard of it, but that it must be a way onto the keep's land he was sure. Rhys closed his eyes for a long moment and dared to unleash those tangled memories, seeking among them for some hint of what he must now find.

The twisted path—it was as if on the inner side of his closed eyelids he could see pictures. A pass, long ago sealed by the force of nature loosed by winter storms. Yet not remaining completely closed now, for time wears away even piles of stone. It had been known in the long ago. Not as easy a path as the one his own people had used for generations but allowing access—at least to a determined band of men.

Earl Florian had always favored sage scholars. Rhys was sure now that, feverishly seeking some way back to his lands, he had drawn upon some very ancient knowledge. But to the Gray One such knowledge was current. There would be another ambush, and Rhys did not doubt that with the Dark power it would again succeed. Unless—

One part of him wanted to skulk along behind that band that had just left the clearing, making sure that they kept on—away from LodenKail. The other part of him felt a pull, a summons to return. The egg had given them a fleeting vision of what was occurring in Raganfors—the egg might not be their greatest aid. He only knew that he could not allow the earl to march to his death if there was anything he could do about it.

So, partly against his will, Rhys turned back. At least he knew where the others were headed now. And if Sanghail also sent a force to join them, they would have some time breaking through the rough land which formed a great part of the barrier in that direction.

But it was the Gray One and that thing of power which lay to the fore of the ranger's mind as he retraced his wandering course. Night was coming fast and the dusk was heavy under the trees.

It was dark by the time he reached the gap and came down

into the bowl. There was no sign of any life save the donkeys and the two goats, though Lopear came trotting to him with a welcoming bray as he headed for the strange entrance to their shelter. Rhys glanced up along the cliff behind, as he had several times in the past few days—there was no gleam of light from any of the concealed window slits. This was truly a well-hidden refuge. They were safe.

18.

Sarita sat cross-legged, staring down in despair. The skin, which was so supple to the touch, seeming near tissue-thin, had proved itself invincible to her scissors, to the edge of her ranger knife, to even tearing with her now broken nails. Yet she *knew* what must be done. Only, please, Lady, she silently pled, give her the knowledge of how to do it.

How could one cut and sew something impervious to any metal blade? It was like one of the old tales where an unfortunate maiden was faced by an insurmountable task. Except in the old tales, some unforeseen aid always arrived.

At least she need not waste time simply sitting and staring at the thing. She could busy her hands at another job. But what was the use of twisting thread which she could not use to sew?

However, she set about smoothing the long locks of hair Rhys had shorn from her head earlier that day and then considered the split bowstrings. Her head felt light. He had done as she ordered and cut as closely to her scalp as he could. She must be a sorry sight, not that that mattered.

Leaving the skin stretched out as they had placed it for measuring, she went now to rummage through their scanty possessions for something to serve as a spool, lighting at last on an article from the treasures they had uncovered: a rod about the length of her hand which had a ridged center. What it might have once been intended for she could not guess, but it did bear some resemblance to a winding spool. It was not of metal, but made of something like polished bone and yellowed by the years.

Sarita discovered that one end could be wedged between two of the close-set stone storage boxes in which most of her own gear now rested. Haltingly at first, and then gaining speed and dexterity as she went, she began her intertwining of hairs and tough gut string, taking the same care at the work as she would have if she wrought the precious gold thread.

As she twisted, she traced back that night vision which had set her to this task. Three of them—Rhys, Valoris, and she—facing a coil of foul evil, each clad in a tight-fitting sheath of Loden-cast skin. This was true dreaming, of that she was entirely sure. What it foretold would come and they must have their defenses ready—if she could make it so.

Scissors could not make the slightest impression, a knife used with force was useless. How then could she shape the garments her dream demanded of her?

In the guildhouse there had been much larger shears, keen of blade, meant for cutting canvas and the heavy materials used for horse trappings. Well, there were none of those to be found here, and she dared not risk breaking her finer blades by force.

She tried to call to mind all she knew of the preparation for work as she had seen it done in the guildhouse. Some of the heavier stretching and cutting had always been done by men. What tools had they used other than the common ones she so easily remembered?

A hunter's knife could slit a hide when used skillfully. She had seen Rhys do that and had learned the knack from his tutoring. And a hide was certainly thicker and stiffer than that skin. But it had already withstood the knife.

Her fingers seemed to move of themselves, twisting and winding her strange thread as she called to mind all the tools she knew. Needles were certainly of no help for cutting; the measure was useless except for its proper job of holding firm the material to be cut. What else remained with her now—? The awl? But that was for marking materials with designs. Sharp as its point was, it had nothing to do with cutting—or had it?

Yes, Dame Argalas had used an awl for cutting once—a tedious piece of work on which she had concentrated with power enough to bring extra wrinkles to her forehead.

There had been a design—a very ancient one, thick with gold

over stitching. The altar cloth of which it was a part had grown too thin and there were small age slits in it. But the frayed silk also backed the emblem, so the use of shears to free it might well cause unraveling, which would doom the heavy design to be burnt for the gold it contained.

Except that this design was a symbol of great power and had hung so long in the sanctuary that the high priestess would have it saved if that could be done. And Dame Argalas had done it! With the point of her awl, she had patiently pricked around the symbol, punching at the silk. Then she had signaled, sitting back on her stool, her hands shaking with exhaustion, while two of the most senior apprentices had carefully taken the far ends of the silk length and lifted. It had come away easily, leaving the symbol intact—cut free with the awl's point.

Carefully Sarita tucked in the end of the thread she had been working with. Though it seemed a very thin chance, she could only try, having nothing else left to do. After placing her loose hair and the bowstrings carefully into the chest and seeing it closed, she got up to go back to the skin, but Valoris came in demanding to be fed and she realized suddenly that she, too, was hungry.

As she prepared their meal, she was impatient to get back to proving whether or not she had the answer to her problem. If she had, how long would it take her to do the necessary cutting using the awl?

She hurriedly ate and saw that Valoris had his share. Their supplies were getting low—that, too, must be taken care of. However, the burning need in her sent her quickly back to work.

Using the heavy measure, she smoothed out a section as flat as she could get it and drew the awl from its loop on her belt. Then she aimed it for the first time down at the scaled length before her and struck at it. The point sank in! She felt the tip touch the stone pavement beneath. Again, she struck just beside the first hole, but this time the point slipped a fraction, did not go straight down but rather skidded along the hard surface and, to her amazement, Sarita saw the skin part along its path as smoothly as silk sheared by the sharpest of blades. It had reached the end of her measure line before she had lost enough surprise to raise it.

To her eyes the awl was as it always had been. There was no

cutting edge on it to account for what had just occurred. Yet the section lay as perfectly cut as if she worked with cloth on the great cutting table in the guildhouse.

Caught up by the excitement of her small success, Sarita went to work furiously, measuring, using the awl to cut, measuring again, fitting piece to piece and examining the joins. She was caught up in such a frenzy of being able to do what she desired that she was unaware of the passing of time until the light which seeped through the walls had begun to dim. Then she sat back on her heels with a sigh.

There were odd scraps of skin left here and there. Valoris had gathered up a handful of those and was engaged in twisting a piece to make a lead for one of his treasured jewel animals, a representation of a quite dangerous-looking quagbear.

Sarita straightened, put her hands to her aching back. She had done all she could do for now. It remained to sort the pieces into piles, each representing one set of clothing, and that was easy enough to do. Now she could return to her threadmaking without the feeling of failure dogging her.

She also gathered the fragments of the skin, having a feeling that nothing must be wasted, though she left Valoris his bit. She ached so—in the guildhouse they were never allowed to sit too long at any task. It was necessary for their health to stretch, to walk around a bit now and then.

Sarita carried the pieces she cut back to her chamber and placed them beside the small ball of thread she had twisted, pushing the heavy lid back over them.

It was then that she realized for the first time Rhys had been gone for a long time. She lit the torch in the room where there was a hearth, which they used for a common room and kitchen. The flickering light was enough to allow her to set up their incongruous spit—a sword so slender that Rhys had marveled that it could be of any use at all, though it did them well enough with a leaper haunch or two impaled on it.

Tired as she was, Sarita felt restless. There was a need—a need to do something she could not put a name to. Valoris was settled happily with his array of toys, the meat was cooked enough to be drawn back from the full heat of the flames. But it was not hunger which moved her now.

She fed the child and saw him settled for the night in his bedroll. Tomorrow she could take her thread into the open and allow him to play outside, which he enjoyed. Now she sat cross-legged in front of the small fire and thought with increasing uneasiness about Rhys. She had been so intent on her struggles with the skin that she had not really listened if he had told her where he was going.

How much could she depend on her vision of the three of them dressed in the skin clothing? Was that a foreseeing of what would really happen, or just a variable which might or might not be in their future? If Rhys never returned from one of these scouts—

She was now fingering the coin pendant he had made for her. Silver was the metal of Light, but how much armor would this be against a well-aimed arrow, a swift sword point?

At last she could stand it no longer. With a last visit to make sure Valoris was fast asleep, she ventured back down to the egg chamber. She had seen Dame Argalas when she had focused her thoughts on the guildwoman—could she use that same power to find Rhys?

However, she was still in the stem-shaped passage when she heard the sound the trapdoor made when opened. Caution bred by the past weeks sent one hand to the hilt of the hunter's sword.

She heard the thump of a body to the floor and stood where she was, waiting. If it were Rhys, he would not hesitate among those chambers but come straight for the passage leading to the quarters above. But there was no sound of movement.

Knowing that she dared not turn her back on the unknown, Sarita crept forward. Now she was at the mouth of the passage. In the faint grayish light which always seemed to cling here, even at night, she could see no movement. Rather—she heard—

In the chamber of the egg! Swiftly, bared steel in hand, she reached the entrance.

It was Rhys there—on his knees before the egg. He was wiping his hands back and forth across his thighs, his eyes fastened on it. Then, as if he had suddenly made up his mind to some action no matter what its consequences might be, he leaned forward and placed both his palms against the egg, leaving a fair distance between them. Sarita was at his shoulder, but he gave no sign that he noticed her arrival.

The whirl of color intensified and then rolled back, as if to frame a picture. It was clear—as clear as her glimpse of Dame Argalas in prison. They were both peering at a camp where figures rolled in blankets made a background for two men still alert and sitting in the full light of the fire.

There was no mistaking the hawk features of Earl Florian. They seemed to have sharpened, or perhaps his cheeks had grown leaner. He wore no polished armor and brilliant surcoat now—his mail had a film of dust on it. He had thrown back the hood over which a battle helm would be fitted, so his dark head was bare. His hair, however, was no longer the silken black of a teeral's wing—there were strands of gray to dim it.

He was talking, gesturing with his hands. But if the egg could bring them this sight, it did not transmit any sound. Sarita caught an impatient exclamation from Rhys and guessed that the ranger was frustrated.

The earl's companion beside the fire also wore mail, but his face was unknown to Sarita. She heard a sudden sound from Rhys as the second man leaned closer to the fire for an instant.

"Ragcor!" It was very plain that Rhys knew that man and there was little good will between them. She saw this Ragcor make some answer to the earl, and then the frame closed in a whirl of fading color.

"No!" Rhys protested. He kept his grip on the egg. "Show me!" he cried like a battle order before he slumped down, his hands falling limply before him. Sarita caught him, or he would have crumpled, steadying him against her own body.

He shook his head back and forth, but did not look at her—he was too intent upon the egg. Twice he tried to raise his hands once more to ovoid, only to be unable to complete the action. She could feel his body trembling, heard his heavy panting as if he had undergone some dire test.

"I must—*see!*" he cried out.

"You will—" Sarita was unsure of her words or even if she uttered the truth. "Rhys." She settled down beside him on the floor now, though she did not remove her hand from where it lay on his shoulder. "Rhys—what do you seek?"

Again he shook his head impatiently and then raised a shaking hand to wipe his sweating face.

"They set a trap—where and how? The Gray One has them mind bound. And Ragcor—if he is the best my lord has to depend on—"

Part of Sarita wanted to shake him into sense, but the rest of her knew that he had put forth what talent he possessed and must now regather his strength.

Rhys' fist struck against his knee. "My lord in the mountains with no sure guide."

"You are sure that they *are* in the mountains?"

For the first time Rhys turned his head to look at her. "Yes—they come by the Twist Road—though why and by what guide—"

"The Twist Road?"

" 'Tis the old way, forgotten in my grandfather's time because of a rock fall there. We believed it closed to any entrance to the valley, though it was inspected from time to time. How—" He stopped suddenly, frowning and turning his head back toward the egg again. "If they can make men their mind slaves, as I have seen this day, then perhaps they can work upon the very stuff of the hills to open the door to their trap!"

Now her grip on him tightened and she dared to shake him. "What have you seen this day?" the girl demanded. "What is this talk of mind slaves and traps?"

He drew a breath which was almost a sigh, then launched into a description of what he had seen while spying upon the wolfhead camp—of the Gray One and of Marken's defeat when he dared to stand against whatever orders had been given.

"The power—it lies in that stone—the black one!" Sarita commented when he had done. Her hand had fallen away from him and she was shivering.

"Yes." He rose slowly, still weak from his farseeing. "And do we have any answer to that?" He walked out of the chamber without looking at her for a reply.

19.

There were no dreams that night. Sarita had stood over Rhys to make sure he ate; his head nodded once, nearly falling into one of the silver plates which she had appropriated from the treasure house for their use. The frustration he had shown earlier was gone and he seemed apathetic. She steered him to the chamber which he had chosen and saw him in his bedroll before she returned to cover the fire for the night and go to her own quarters.

Firmly she set her mind on the work which had busied her most of the day and refused to allow Rhys' tale any room in her thoughts. Before she rolled into her own sleep nest, she looked once more on Valoris.

How safe was he even here? That thought also she put firmly from her. And sleep did come.

Valoris was first up in the morning, as often happened, yet he did not play with his animals in the usual fashion but came to Sarita, pulling at her blanket until she looked up groggily.

"Lady—Lady come!"

Lady? She was still sleep dazed, whom did he mean?

"Saree, Lady come!" He tugged harder at the covers until she sat up.

"Lady—" His hands moved out in a gesture which seemed to encompass all around them. "Lady here!"

He was already at the door of their chamber while Sarita pulled on her clothing and tried to make some sort of order of the few locks remaining on her shorn head. He was out of sight by the time she reached the large hall, but the toy quadbear lay abandoned at the door of the Audience Chamber. Lady! How could he mean—?

She sped to the door. There was the light on those thrones again, and Valoris was there, walking sturdily toward them. Sarita's fear of the melted one flared, and she hurried forward to catch Valoris' shirt in a firm grip.

"No!" Valoris instantly fought against her. "bad Saree—go Lady! Go Lady now!"

"Let him come!"

The voice rang not in her ears but in her mind. Before Sarita's eyes a silver mist gathered on the intact throne. Speechlessly she obeyed, and Valoris scrambled up on the dais to the very foot of that seat. Did she or did she not see a form lean forward, a movement through the air as if a hand reached down to touch the child's head?

"This one," again the voice sounded in her mind, "is sealed to Us, daughter, and he shall be a faithful liege all his life. Get you to your craft, for the time soon comes when its fruits will be needed. Blessings on what you do and the why of its making."

The mist was gone—if she had truly seen it. But, as Valoris turned away from the now empty throne and came down to her, she saw something very strange. One of the crisp curls which lay against his forehead was gleaming silver, much as if it were wrought of metal.

Still bemused, Sarita followed the child, who pattered ahead, pausing to retrieve his quadbear at the doorway. She met Rhys as he burst out of his chamber and into the outer hall. He had not stopped to put on boots, his clothing was awry from having slept in it, and he stood looking at her, his eyes wide, a grim set to his mouth.

"What has happened?" he demanded, and caught her roughly by the arm, swinging her around to face him squarely. "What walks—" Though there was a shadow of what might be fear upon him, there was also the strength withstand it.

"She—" Sarita found herself nearly stuttering and took a firmer grip on herself. "*She* came—" And she launched into as plain a description as she could give of what had happened in the Audience Chamber.

Some of the tension went out of him, and he passed his hand over his stubbled face. "I felt—" he mumbled. "Why—?" There was frustration and a note of irritation in his voice. "Why have we been chosen to be liegemen of—of—shadows?"

"You said there were those of old who had talents," the girl reminded him, but inwardly she ached with that same question. Why was she, a guildswoman's daughter, happy with her insulated life, being pitched into matters far beyond the world she knew?

"Not talents," Rhys continued, following some line of thought on his own, "but burdens." He had kept his hold on her, and now his fingers bit into her flesh until she winced; he noticed and loosed his grip. "Your pardon—it is only that I feel as much Lopear under a pack—that I bear another's burdens whether I will or no." He shook himself as if he was attempting to throw off such bindings.

"Rhy—Ryyy—" Valoris was pulling at the edge of the ranger's jerkin, looking up into his face. "Lady—" In this dull light the silver curl appeared to have a luminescence of its own.

"Yes." Rhys stooped and caught up the boy. "The Lady—well, we will march by Her orders no matter what those may be. I with weapons to hand and you," he looked at Sarita again, "with your needle, though what good that may be—"

Sarita had already turned toward the hearth room. She was finding strength in a regular plan for the day. "Go wash and show me a clean face," she said, smiling. "Take our lordling, he is in good need, too. If we are to work out some task, we'll do it with full stomachs and properly clean."

His laugh matched hers. "Listen, lordling," he had swung the boy up on his shoulders, "we have our orders. And we shall bring you sharp appetites," he warned as they separated.

Sarita went to wash her own face. Unluckily there was no comb to put her roughly cut hair in order. To keep it out of her eyes, she crammed on a golden circlet from the treasure box and tucked in all the ends she could. Then she was back to the fire and their remaining supplies.

They would certainly need more of those and soon. Surely no task looming over them from the unknown would make it unneedful for them to eat and sleep. They might be now commanded by shadows, but they still had bodies which must be kept alert and satisfied.

She pointed out the lack of supplies to Rhys when he came back with Valoris, his face scrupulously shaven with a knife edge, his hair sleeked back. He had taken time to change his shirt and breeches for ones she had washed down by the lake two days ago.

"Yes, I set snares a day ago on the far ridge—there were rock fowl thereabouts. Also, I saw a clump of fiddle ferns down near the lake—"

"You will see it no longer," she retorted. "I harvested them two days ago, when I washed our clothes. There are reeds there, also— what of their roots?"

Her experience of the early morning almost faded as she went briskly about hearthwife duties. "It will lie on you," she said suddenly, confronting him with her fists on her hips and her jaw a little outthrust, "to do the harvesting. I have this." One of her hands slid around to thump against the pouch on her belt. "We have but little time."

Rhys looked back at her over his shoulder from where he crouched by the fire, then he continued to watch the spit, where a leaper haunch sputtered and spat grease at the flames below.

"Yes." His lightness of spirit had vanished and he answered her somberly. "That I also know."

She did not watch him leave the bowl valley as she usually did. Rather, from the moment she had washed and stacked their plates, she set about the task she had begun the day before. Since the suit for Valoris was the smallest and he was present to have it tried on if necessary, she brought up the lightest bundle of skin pieces. A sudden guess led to experiments. The leftover bits could be sliced thinly and also twisted with hair. Which was good, since the supply of bowstrings was limited. Now she went to winding with a vigor, working as fast as she could without stinting the proper tight smoothness of each strand.

At length she believed she had enough to begin her task and she opened her needle case. There was no choice—only one of the larger-eyed bone needles could be used. However, remembering the need for the awl, she wondered if each hole would have to be separately punched. Almost gingerly she took up two lengths of skin, ready to use the lacing stitches she thought best.

However, the skin, which had so obstructed scissors and knife blade, gave way to the bone needle. In a few moments she fell into the rhythm of work which she knew of old, and her tension eased. There was no sandclock to mark the hours, and she was not aware that time passed until Valoris again came to be fed. Then she was inwardly impatient, wanting to get back to her work, though moving about eased her aching back.

There was a fitting during the afternoon, and the boy was unusually patient as she shifted and did some of the actual sewing while it was on his body. She had devised as a pattern a pair of breeches with a long-sleeved shirt. In fact, the sleeves protruded over the hands and could be draw in to form mittens, while there was a hood on the shoulders which in turn could cover the whole head, leaving only holes for eyes and mouth. Why she had chosen such a pattern Sarita did not know—only that it must be done.

She was surprised herself at the fruits of her industry, for she was ready for a final fitting by the time the light was fading. She had taken the last important stitch just in time, for her thread was near to its end and soon, she must twist more.

"What have we here?" Sarita was badly startled by that sudden question, but Valoris did not seem surprised. He put up his hands quickly and pulled the hood over his head and then jumped at Rhys where he stood in the doorway, uttering a sound he probably considered to be a growl.

The ranger looked from the child to the girl in amazement. Then he stooped to meet Valoris on his level.

"Loden—the Loden—" He cowered back as if in fear and Valoris' laughter rang out.

"Loden!" He agreed and shuffled in a kind of war dance about the stooping ranger. "It is Loden!" He waved his hands high.

Rhys again looked to the girl. "Sarita." He so seldom used her name that it seemed doubly important when he did. "This is strange—do we now put on new skins?"

Slowly she nodded. "Such is the task set me, Rhys. There is a reason even if we do not understand it now."

So time sped. In the evenings by the hearth she twisted the

thread that she used by day. She was so busy, she was hardly aware when Rhys came and went—save there was always food of one kind or another to hand. He took Valoris with him when he scouted for growing things in the bowl, and one evening, as Sarita settled the child in bed, the boy was full of the events of that day: Rhys has been building a house for Berry, Briar, and the donkeys and he, Valoris, had helped by carrying even big, big stones.

When Sarita went back to her nightly task of thread winding, she asked about this, and for a long moment Rhys did not answer. When he did, it was with his old habit of picking his words carefully.

"We shall be leaving here—for I must go and I cannot leave you and the lordling behind—also I know that you have a part to play. But we cannot take the animals, for when the time comes we must move swiftly. There is good grazing land here, and if they have a shelter against storms, they can perhaps winter—if we do not return."

"Where do we go?" Her hands were still busy with the thread, but he had startled her out of her preoccupation.

"Earl Florian comes—he must not meet with death as did the others. I have been to the egg again, Sarita," he ended, like one making a confession.

"And you have seen what?" she demanded sharply.

"What must be done. Look here." He took a charred end of a stick from the fire and began to draw on the floor. "This is where the trail enters the valley, less than a half day's journey from here. They will, I think, allow him to come in, perhaps as much as a day's march, before they close their trap. I—I have seen what must be done!"

His face was in shadow, for the flicker of the fire was low, but the note in his voice was that of one swearing an oath. He reached behind him, and she saw that his quiver of arrows lay there. Out from among the shafts he drew two. Even in the limited light they gleamed.

"Silver—" he said, running a finger along the edge of one head. "This—this will serve us or we fail."

"You have seen—ahead—?" She wet her lips with her tongue tip. Why should he not have done so when her dream had guided her to her labor?

"I could not see the end," he returned, "only what was to happen, so that I might be prepared. But there is never any true end until it comes. For a man may fail or succeed by his own strength of will, and so he cannot see the consequences of what he would do. Yes, I have seen what must be done. The Gray One will be among the ambushers and he will carry—"

"That mind blinding thing!" Sarita interrupted. "Silver—is silver then the true answer to that?"

"If what I have seen is true—yes. Tomorrow I must begin to practice, for the outcome will lie on my bow skill."

Much against her will, Sarita was drawn from her own now feverish hours of labor to aid in that practice for a space, first tossing plates in the air, then smaller discs they had found. She marveled at his skill, but she noted that he did not use the silver-tipped arrows, rather his usual shafts. And now he did not miss. She began holding an object some distance from him. The first time or so she played target, she quaked within, but she would not allow him to guess that. However, it seemed to her that his skill increased with every shaft he let fly.

She had always heard that the rangers were expert archers. Yet still she was amazed at his accuracy, and she wondered if he had not held a special place among his fellows.

However, she rebelled at last, saying that she *must* finish what she had to do. Though he looked as if he would argue with her, he let her go without saying anything.

Her own work was nearly completed. She had tried on and adjusted the suit she had cut for herself. There remained only the one for Rhys. That evening she gave him the skin-tight covering, and he emerged from his chamber a figure which startled her, for he had drawn down the hood. They would never perhaps know what the true Loden shape was—they could only guess. But for anyone who had not seen the original skin, here indeed was a monster such as might awaken awe and fear.

There were some lacings to tighten as he stood patiently. But while she was doing so, Valoris came charging from the other side of the room. In his hand Sarita saw, to her horror, one of the small, jewel-hilted knives she had discovered and had hoped were successfully hidden, she threw out an arm, but he avoided her. In doing so the boy stumbled, the knife thudding home against Rhys' thigh. Only—the blade rebounded with enough force to throw it out of the child's hand, and there was no sign of any tear in the scaled length.

Sarita sat motionless, still shaking at the thought of what might have happened. Rhys spoke first:

"Now we know." He picked up the knife and deliberately aimed it at his own breast. Once more the point made no impression on the skin which covered him. "Armor past belief!" There was awe in his voice. "Truly we are favored."

20.

It had been raining when they left the LodenKail, and it continued to rain throughout the day, even into the night, a steady downpour. So they had put the skin suits to another test. Even under periods of heightened downpour, they shed water. Rhys and Sarita each shouldered a small pack covered with the oiled material that kept their scanty rations and Rhys' bowstrings dry. At the last minute Sarita had shyly produced a length of the twisted hair and skin in payment for the strings he had sacrificed for her thread. After a trial or two, Rhys had been highly pleased by its service.

Here in the heights the ranger took a high peak for their guide and they angled toward it. Though he ranged ahead at intervals, they moved at a pace which at first Valoris could keep; later Sarita carried the child in the now almost too small back sling.

She was plodding stolidly ahead in what might have been midafternoon when her talent awoke. Rhys had made one of his disappearances and she stayed where she was for the moment, not wishing to enter any trap.

The ranger slid into view and Sarita, looking at his scaled body, that bulbous hood pulled down against the storm, thought he certainly made a monstrous appearance.

"Wolfheads," he told her, "with a backing of liegemen wearing Sanghail's colors. They are lying up along the trail end. It is as I thought, they will allow the earl well into the land before they close on him."

"Why does not Earl Florian send out scouts?"

Rhys looked grim. "How do we know what games the Gray One

has played? He may not have to face men directly before he sets his mind seal on them. We rangers rode blindly into that ambush— can we believe the earl is better prepared now? He may not even guess the nature of the true enemy."

"What can be done?" Sarita eased Valoris out of the sling. There was a light overhang of rock to one side which offered shelter of a sort. She pushed the boy under it and knelt down just under the overhang.

Rhys strode up and down, frowning. Twice he paused and looked up at the heights ahead. The vegetation here was sparse, some of it standing in heavy clumps, the rest laced over outcroppings of rock.

"When they close their trap," he said slowly, coming to drop down beside her, "then—" His hand went out in a curious sweeping gesture. "See, Sarita, they have been mind set upon a special task— all their attention must be held to that, for if they are allowed freedom of extra thought they may win freedom of all. They have no scouts out except to the fore. Here they lie—" He drew his belt knife and began to draw lines in the soft earth under the overhang.

"Here they lie in waiting. This is the trail—it is rough and very narrow. The earl's men need to string out like one of your threads in order to advance. But these who lie in wait will not expect—"

Sarita nodded. "They would not expect an attack from the rear." But she looked at the child and then to Rhys with something of a challenge. "We are two—two and a half. The little lordling, he must not be harmed. Yet this you cannot do alone. So will you work around these rats waiting to easily take their cheese and warn the earl—?"

Rhys slowly shook his head. "The lay of the land is against me. No. Sarita, who stands behind you now?"

She gave a small gasp and turned her head, half expecting to see some danger, for the prick of peril was steady now. She saw only the range of heights down which they had come.

"LodenKail," Rhys said slowly. "Monster's land. The wolfheads have never ranged its slopes. And who are we—?" His eyes met hers squarely and held.

Sarita's heart began to beat faster. Her mouth seemed to dry of itself as she got out the words.

"Loden! But we are—not—" Her hands slipped along the rain-sleeked scales which covered her. "The cast skin—it was from one such as we—"

"Do they know that?" Rhys nodded toward the way ahead. "There has never, in any tale I heard, been any mention of how the Loden might appear to those who invaded its lands. Nor was there any word that the Loden was solitary of its kind. Those wolf-heads might well expect monsters, so . . ."

So this was the true meaning of the dream which had set her to her labors these past days—that sight of the three of them standing against a rising dark, clad in the skin of one who had once defeated that same darkness.

"But Valoris—" she protested.

"We shall put the child behind us when we move. But we cannot leave him in this wilderness. I like it no better than you do, yet this is our only chance. We have until morning, I am sure. The earl will not try to work his way down through that last broken land in the dark. And by the looks of those waiting, they have settled in well."

They ate from the supplies they carried, and then the three of them hunched closely together under the rock. It seemed to Sarita that the rain fell with less force; perhaps the storm was close to an end.

She cuddled Valoris against her, but her own sleep that night was only a few short dozes from which she awoke confused, aware of her aching body, then more sharply of what might lie before them. Looked at with cold sense, Rhys' plan was sheer folly; still, she was certain that they were going to proceed just as he had foretold. She longed to ask him if he had visited the egg before leaving—had he been given some message he had not chosen to share with her?

There was an odd luminescence to their suits, equal perhaps to some of the fungi of the forest. She could see his features plainly. His jaw was firmly set, the mouth above it thin, and there was a frown line deepened between his black brows. It seemed to her now that she had known him always, that he was the bloodkin she had never had. Yes, she must lay her trust on him. And now in her came a strange feeling of peace, fleeting but plain, even as she had known it in that ancient audience hall of LodenKail.

The rain stopped before morning, but there was a mist which curled in thick eddies and Rhys stood surveying that.

"Is it to the good or ill?" he apparently asked himself rather than her. "No mind, we must move on."

They left their packs behind, Rhys merely taking with him his dry bowstrings, which he now placed within the breast of his suit. Since they had started this trek Valoris had been quiet and biddable, almost unnaturally so. He had asked no questions and eaten without question what they had given him.

Now he moved forward and caught Rhys' left hand, reaching back to link also with Sarita.

"Go—go—!" his excitement was growing. How much was he part of this? Sarita wondered. The Lady had certainly blessed him and they were, in some way, about Her business.

Thus they entered the mists and the glow born of the skins appeared to deepen. Rhys moved without any hesitation. Sarita felt it also—that drawing. Whatever lay ahead was meant to be their own fate.

"Haaa!"

Rhys stopped short, jerking Sarita and the child closer to him. The voice had come out of the mists before them.

"How're we goin' t' get any range in this here soup?"

"Quit blatin' off yur mouth, Smeek. We'll get 'em right—"

The second speaker did not finish. There was something quivering in the very air about them. The mist was whirling, being tugged from one side and then the other. But this was no act of nature. Sarita bit her lip. It was so strong—that nearing of evil. Power was being used, such power as she could not understand.

The world before them was clearing fast. They were standing at the top of a low ridge and there was a thickening of growth below them. But, as plainly as if she had been afforded some power of her own, Sarita could pick out the men lying in wait there as if they lay completely in the open.

"A-comin'—" Perhaps that was meant as a whisper, but the warning reached the three on the ridge as if it had been shouted aloud.

Now the girl could see the thread of an ancient trail, much overshadowed by growth. There was movement, too. She caught a glimpse of a travel-worn surcoat: the advance rank of the earl's party was in view. And—her throat tightened—they were working their way ahead with no more suspicion of their surroundings than if they had been marching to the keep in peace time. Were they mind blinded?

"Harrroooow—" The throat-straining cry broke from right beside her. Rhys stood steady, his hands fitting arrow to string before he let fly. There was a commotion among those who were hidden. Sarita heard someone give a choking cry.

The men filing down the trail had halted, heads turned in their direction.

"Harrooow—!" Again Rhys shouted, and shot. The men in the trail were pulling quickly back. Now one of the wolfheads staggered up from the brush, his hands clutching at an arrow which had pierced him through. Sarita plucked at one of the pouches on her belt and rolled a stone into her hand to load her sling. She could see someone moving now and let fly.

The target jerked and fell. Whether she had done much damage she could not tell, but at least the man was not moving anymore.

Rhys shot with the steady precision he might have shown aiming at the butts on a feast day. And he was making every arrow count.

Men broke from the cover of the ambush, some of them tangled with the earl's forces in hand-to-hand battle, but three of them had turned to face the ridge. One, a small, rat-faced man, dropped his sword and staggered back.

"Loden!" he screamed. His two followers stood uncertainly while Rhys picked one off neatly and sent the other to the ground with a shaft through his thigh.

But arrows were now rising in turn from the wolfheads. Sarita swept Valoris behind her and then staggered from the force of a blow against her midsection which nearly sent the breath out of her. A broken arrow lay on the rocks below her. She saw Rhys, too, take a step back as one of the enemies' arrows struck him high in the shoulder. For a moment his own bow wavered, and she knew that he was troubled by the force of the blow even if it had not pierced the skin.

Something bright skimmed through the air and Sarita's arm swept up, to be rendered numb by the thud of another arrow. Her sling was now useless to her, but she set her teeth and forced her fingers instead around the hilt of the hunting sword at her belt.

It was not another arrow which set her head spinning. Rather, it was a mind blast heavy enough to darken the world before her eyes. When she could see again, that gray shape, seemingly risen out of the very ground, stood looking upslope at them.

Hands came forth from long, full sleeves, hands as thin as the bones which formed them, as gray as the robe. They came together, and clutched in talon fingers was a mass of darkness.

"Do not look!" Rhys' voice was as loud as a death scream. She saw him moving—slowly—so slowly. Perhaps he was caught in that same rising web of smothering power. But he had his bow up, he had an arrow nocked. She saw a flash of light streak downward.

However, Rhys was wavering from side to side, fighting some compulsion which was drawing him.

"No!" She pushed across his path, her body seeming leaden heavy. He crashed into her and sent them both rolling down the slope aways. Sarita pushed herself up a little.

There stood the Gray One. In his hands pulsed the ball of blackness. She must not look! That warning was her first thought. But shaking in the ball, as if the monstrous thing was trying to rid itself of that burden, was the silver-headed arrow Rhys had shot.

She could hear a droning deep in her head. The Gray One was striving to loose his power. At the same time he was gliding toward them. Could the Loden skin hold against such an evil? Silver— silver! Her hand was fumbling at her belt, her shaking fingers closed about the awl. Silver . . .

The Gray One loomed over them now. He stretched his arms so that quivering mass of black was directly over Rhys. The girl saw that the ranger's hood had been shoved back during his roll down-slope—there was no skin to protect him. His eyes were fixed in a set stare on the pulsing blackness.

Sarita gave a desperate heave upward. She had very little time for aiming as she cried aloud:

"Lady—Loden—!"

The awl entered the mass. Her hand fell away, but not before a freezing chill caught at her fingers, crooking them, then spreading up to her wrist.

But the mass—in her head was a thin, mind-splitting scream which seemed to almost drive her beyond the bounds of reason. Then there was a flare, not of black but of clear silver, as if the Light had gulped down that greedy blackness.

There came another cry—this time from the Gray One. He half turned, as if to run, but he never took his first stride. Instead his body wavered like a ribbon caught in breeze. He crumpled down to his knees, then fell forward as Rhys got stiffly to his feet and reached down to draw Sarita up with him. It almost appeared that the evil one was a penitent surrendering to his enemy, fallen at their feet.

"Loden!" There were shrieks and cries, and the sound of blows. Sarita held tightly to Rhys as they stood looking in dull amazement at the Gray One. The garment was falling in upon itself, crumbling as if there was no body within to fill it. And now the gray fabric itself began to fray.

Rhys was nearly swept from his feet again by a blow aimed by a sword. The wolfheads—no, these were soldiers, wearing Var colors.

"Kill!" That was a screamed order. Again the sword thrust came, this time sending Sarita reeling backward.

"Sareee—Sareee—" Faintly she heard the high voice calling her.

"Get back!" Her lips shaped the words, but she did not have energy enough to shout them. Rhys— The ranger still moved as if he were caught in a bog mud, and his head was vulnerable, with the hood well back. Those ringing them in, having tried twice to bring them down, had withdrawn a little now.

Down the slope behind them came a small body that careened into Sarita. She caught him up tightly for a moment, and then swept Valoris behind her for what protection her own body might give him. Before her an ax was raised, and Rhys was standing dumbly, weaving a little, unable to protect himself from the death over his head.

Hastily the girl clawed back her own hood and then brought Valoris from behind her and did the same for the child.

"*Look!*" she screamed. "This is the young lordling. Would you kill those who are liege to Var?"

21.

Weapons were still threatening them, but the soldiers were no longer gripped by battle rage. Rather they eyed the three they had encircled with a new wariness, though Sarita thought she could read little belief of her claim. Surely they did not believe that they had taken monsters!

Into the rocky clearing came another man. With an impatient hand he swept off the helm he wore.

"Fadda!" Valoris was running, and the soldiers parted to let him through. He threw himself forward straight into the arms of the man who had gone down on one knee to welcome him.

"Valoris!" That cry was as loud as a battle rally as Earl Florian held his son in tight embrace. Then he loosed the child and held him farther away, studying him, running hands over the scaled suit—as if he sought for some injury, as if he could not believe in this meeting.

"Fadda!" The boy's arms went up about the man's neck. "Fadda—you camed!"

"Indeed I did," the earl assured him hoarsely, but now, having made sure of the child's well-being, he looked to the other two his men still guarded. His eyes fastened on Rhys; there was a momentary frown as if Earl Florian searched his memory. Then, rising to his feet and swinging Valoris up to his shoulder, he approached, his men falling back to give him room.

"You are . . ." Again that trace of frown, and then the earl nodded. "You are Rhys Rogarson of my rangers."

Rhys' hand swept up into the breast salute of a fighting man to his commander. The lethargy which had held him was gone.

"Yes, my lord," he answered crisply.

But Earl Florian's gaze had already gone on to Sarita. She thought of her shock of untidy hair, of the fact that she had never had dealings at Var with the earl—that had been for Dame Argalas. No—he could not know her.

He was looking puzzled again. "Halda? But Halda . . ." he said, as if he expected her somehow to turn into that trusted nurse.

"She is dead, my lord." Sarita found her voice. "I am Sarita Magasdaughter, apprentice to Dame Argalas—or was." She drew a deep breath, for that identity seemed so far in the past that it no longer mattered. "Or so I was when Var-The-Outer fell."

"They set an ambush for you—" Rhys broke in as if he wished to make sure that threat was gone.

"Which did not work. We heard your ranger's call, Rhys Rogarson. But I think more than wolfheads and some traitor scum waited us here. What I saw . . ."

He turned his head to look at the ground. Sarita could still barely distinguish the rags of the gray robe from the trampled soil.

Now the earl looked again to them. "It would seem that there is a tale here which must be told, and soon, for we do not know what perils we march against. Yost—" One of those in the circle lowered his weapon and saluted. "Send out scouts. Why—" there was a look of puzzlement now on the earl's thin and furrowed face "—did we not have such before? What power summoned us as tamely as sheep to the butcher?"

Gently he set Valoris on the ground, though he kept one hand on the boy's shoulder as if his son would disappear again. He edged toward what was left of the Gray One.

"Do not—!"

"My lord, take care!"

Both Rhys' and Sarita's warnings ran out together. The earl glanced at them.

"Be very sure that I shall. There has been a spewing of evil across this land, and it would seem that some drop of such spittal struck here. Such as this one have had their way in Raganfors. Did he twist our minds?" he appealed to the ranger and the girl. "Is

that why we marched without thought to what could have been
our deaths?"

Rhys nodded vigorously. "He—he had an object of power, lord,
that leached men's wills out of them."

Earl Florian stooped now. Sarita gasped—he must not touch
what lay there. She did not know how the Dark could spread, but
there must be caution taken. However, what the earl picked up was
an arrow.

The head was blackened, melted out of shape, as if it had been
held in a strong, burning fire. The shaft was charred. Still holding
the arrow, the earl now kicked at something in the soil and a mis-
shapen lump rolled into plainer sight.

"Your weapons ranger, mistress?" he asked.

"Silver, lord," Rhys returned quickly. "Of old it was said that
silver would be the only metal to harm some of the Dark ones. I
had silver heads on two of my arrows.

"But yours, I think, mistress, was no arrow." The earl looked
at Sarita.

"No." For the first time the full wonder of what had happened
in those wild seconds when the Gray One would have bent his full
power on Rhys shook her. "It was my awl, a tool of my craft. But
it was also silver."

The earl laughed. "An arrow and an awl—and what is left of
my force saved so. We must hear the full of your tale, ranger, guilds-
daughter. But I think we shall not pause for it here."

Rhys looked at Sarita and she gave a small nod.

"Lord," he said, "we can offer you a safe camp as well as a tale."

"Where?"

Rhys turned a little to point up and back toward the bare peak
of LodenKail. "There, lord."

Now came a murmur from the men. Someone said, "monster,"
and Sarita answered:

"Lord, do you still call us monsters? Yet—" her hand went out
and sleeked down the side of her body, brushing away the bits of
soil caught in the scales "—yet we serve both the Loden and the
Lady. What we wear is Loden skin."

The murmur from the men came louder now.

Again the earl laughed, almost as if their words had freed him from some burden.

"So be it—and where would you lead us?"

"To the Loden's lair," Sarita answered promptly. "For there safety lies."

"Well enough. We must have a base from which we can scout. It is true Sanghail has set his foot here?" He demanded that of Rhys as if expecting such news.

"It is true."

"My—my lady?" That question came harsh and quick.

"She is gone, my lord," Sarita answered, again in her mind the picture of that green-cloaked body spattered with red, rolling from where the horseman tossed her. "No one else that we know of came out of the keep. Halda was struck down by a traitoress, but first gave Valoris to me and showed me a passage in the walls to take him out."

The earl was not looking at her now, rather staring at the slope of mountain as if he could only see some painful tangle of his own thoughts.

"So be it. At least you have saved this much of Var." His hand touched Valoris' head. "And debts of blood will be paid, even if they are a long time in coming. No, set us on the trail to this lair of a monster whom you have seemed to have tamed."

Meanwhile, his party made sure of the wolfheads and of a handful of liveried liegemen who had set the ambush. His men had gained in spirit from the destruction of the object of Dark power and the death of its master. Free of the invisible control, they found themselves as if newly awakened. But the wolfheads and their allies, deprived of the Gray One, had become near artless—many of them dying without a blade laid to them.

They traveled at a fast pace, for the earl seemed determined to make sure that they would win to the promised refuge as quickly as possible. Rhys knew that he and Sarita, as well as Valoris, were still surreptitiously watched because of their suits. For the first time the ranger was aware how much the tight covering revealed of the girl's body, though she did not appear to be aware of the fact. How could he have never noticed how pretty she was?

The earl kept them both close to him and they spilled out their

own story as they went. He made no comment until Sarita spoke of
the invulnerability of the scaled suits and how she had used the
shed skin to fashion them.

"But of the Loden there was no sign?" the earl asked then.

"None," she replied. "Save—there is a feeling, my lord. It may
touch you and your men also: a feeling of loss, sadness—I think
that the Loden is truly gone and we are the poorer for it."

He seemed to be thinking deeply and asked no more questions.
They halted and ate, scouts reported an empty land, as if the enemy
had been so sure of their ambush that they sent only the men for
that. Them—and the Gray One.

When they reached the gap and came down into the bowl, it
was mid-morning of the next day. A racous bray was their first greeting as Lopear came trotting toward them. He was answered by whin-
nies from the dozen mounts the earl's party had brought. The horses
had to be carefully led up the rough way, but now they tugged at
their reins, the lake and the rich grass temptingly laid out before
them.

"So." The earl was keenly studying what lay about him. "This is
Loden Lair. To that one we give thanks for shelter. But perhaps—"
He was smiling now; once more Valoris rode on his shoulder, the
sun glinting in rainbow brightness from the skin covering on his
small body. "But perhaps we shall bring back life to a legend. Have
we not three Lodens—not just one—to give us company?"

Sarita rubbed the fingers of her right hand with her left. Since
she had struck that blow with the awl, they tended to cramp unex-
pectedly, but she refused to believe that such a wound was
permanent.

"Berry!" Valoris pointed to the goat. "Berry come—"

Then he spoke slowly and carefully, as if he must repeat an
important lesson and be sure he had it right:

"Loden want Val, Saree, Ry—Fadda—Loden good."

Then it seemed to Sarita that the sadness which clung here was
lightening, as the sun drew away a mist. She did not know what the
future might hold, but they had knowledge—such knowledge as had
not been known in this land for generations of her blood—and
certainly the prospect to learn even more. Here, indeed, was a lair,

and Sanghail and those like him might well find that LodenKail was about to give forth Lodens once again.

She was startled—her thought had been matched by a sudden knowledge. Rhys . . . Yes, there would come such Lodens out of this lair as the Gray Ones could not foresee, strong in power as they were. And she—she would be a part of it—and Rhys, and the men now trailing with their mounts down toward the lake.